Spine of Steel

Andrea Jenelle

Willow Creek Publishing

Copyright © 2025 by Andrea Jenelle

All rights reserved.

No part of this publication may be reproduced, distributed, or transmitted in any form or by any means, including photocopying, recording, or other electronic or mechanical methods, without the prior written permission of the publisher, except as permitted by U.S. copyright law. This included the use of any of this material, or any portion thereof, for the training, synchronization or adaptation by or for artificial intelligence. For permission requests, contact andreajenelle@andreajenelleromance.com

The story, all names, characters, and incidents portrayed in this production are fictitious. No identification with actual persons (living or deceased), places, buildings, and products is intended or should be inferred.

Book Cover Design by Willow Creek Publishing

Book Cover Photo: Deposit Photos

1st edition 2025

This one's for Gypsy.

My grandmother was 101 when she died in 2012. She vividly remembered the day women were granted the right to vote. From the time she turned eighteen she voted in every single election, no matter how big or small. She was a poll worker for over sixty years, and a fierce believer in democracy and equal opportunity.

Contents

1. Chapter One — 1
2. Chapter Two — 10
3. Chapter Three — 23
4. Chapter Four — 31
5. Chapter Five — 38
6. Chapter Six — 48
7. Chapter Seven — 55
8. Chapter Eight — 63
9. Chapter Nine — 74
10. Chapter Ten — 83
11. Chapter Eleven — 91
12. Chapter Twelve — 104

13.	Chapter Thirteen	117
14.	Chapter Fourteen	126
15.	Chapter Fifteen	133
16.	Note to Readers	137
	About the author	140
	Also by Andrea	141

Chapter One

Diogenes Castellano was an arrogant, self-righteous ass. Perry knew beyond the shadow of a doubt that he was the single-most infuriating man on the planet.

But sometimes Pericles Trenton stared at his mouth and forgot her name. And how to speak.

And Pericles Trenton was never speechless because crafting words was her stock in trade. For the last five years, she'd single-handedly been running the Willow Creek Crier. She was the reporter, the writer, the editor-in-chief and primary hawker.

She was also the secret translator and purveyor of a series of scandalous Italian memoirs about the lives of sixteenth-century Venetian courtesans and their escapades.

Her tongue-tied behavior around the man who'd tormented her since childhood was nonsensical. In every other area of her life she was firmly in control of her emotions and her reactions. But Dio unraveled her until she felt like a gormless nitwit - captivating her in some devilish display of power she couldn't make heads or tails of. When her brother's tall, bespectacled best friend swiped a stray drop of applejack from the rim of his glass with his tongue, or closed his eyes as he wrapped his mouth around a spoonful of chocolate mousse, Perry was rendered both speechless and witless.

She wanted to leap across the table and grab his chin. She wanted to press her thumb in the much too intriguing divot in the center of it.

Soup tureen be damned.

She wanted to clamber over the half-empty platter of roast and lick away the spot of chocolate caught in his dimple. Because it was slowly driving her mad.

She wanted to toss the half-full pitcher of peppered gravy in his direction, and then reach across the table and lift his glasses from his face on the pretense of cleaning them. Which she would accomplish by sitting down beside him and lifting her skirts so she could use her petticoat. Doing that would bare her ankle - and she hoped the innocuousness of it would upend him the same way she was upended by the way his throat bobbed when he laughed. Every time he let loose with a gusty whoop she had to bite her tongue so she wouldn't lean forward and bite his Adam's apple instead.

Their fathers had been the best of friends at Harvard. Dio's ancestors were farmers and vintners under the patronage of Jefferson, and the Trentons were the descendants of Scots-Irish immigrants in the mid eighteenth-century. The two men found they both abhorred slavery and were staunch abolitionists. They fought alongside one another in the Union Army and the bonds they formed on the battlefield were so pronounced, Dio's father had followed his friend from Appomattox to Willow Creek.

Diogenes, or Dio as her brothers called him, had been a fixture in her house for as long as she could remember.

That had been all well and good. Until the summer she turned twenty-one.

The annual baseball game after the town picnic could become quite boisterous. Her two brothers were dead-ringer pitchers and even though her mother said it wasn't genteel, Perry always ended up behind the home plate as the catcher.

That summer, at that game, Dio went down in a pile of dust when her brother Archimedes threw a wild pitch. Perry had crashed to her knees, and when he'd opened his eyes, she'd noticed how velvety soft they were behind his mangled spectacles. Like the ears of the pet rabbit she'd carried around everywhere she went when she was seven.

And then she noticed his lips. The firm upper one with the very pronounced bow, just hidden by his mustache, and the plush, ripe bottom one like a juicy strawberry that was framed by his dark beard.

For the last five years, she hadn't been able to stop noticing his lips.

She was noticing them now. The way they scraped against his fork and melded around his spoon.

"What are you staring at, termagant?" He said around a mouthful of boiled potatoes.

She wasn't about to confess why she was transfixed. "Do you have to scrape the fork against your teeth every single time you take a bite? It borders on uncouth."

He gave her an unrepentant grin and scraped it again. "But these are excellent boiled potatoes."

She didn't want to laugh. Or smile. But she couldn't help herself.

"Thankfully, as annoying as you can be, you are no Mr. Collins."

He gave her one of the rare smiles that just turned up the corner of his beguiling lips. "I see your opinion of me has improved since you were fifteen. You called me a lout then because I wouldn't swim into the middle of the pond and tow your sinking canoe back to shore. You claimed even Mr. Collins would have expended the effort - if only to ingratiate himself."

Perry was never going to betray how far he'd moved up in the ranks of her esteem. She set her spoon beside her empty bowl and narrowed her eyes at him. "As I said, you're no Mr. Collins," she smirked. "But you're no Darcy either. You're more like Wickham."

He set his own spoon down and returned her glare. "I beg your pardon?"

His voice rose at the end of the question and Perry gleefully reveled in the fact her insult had gotten under his skin.

Archie thumped Dio between the shoulder blades. "Are you frowning at my sister again?"

Her brother found it hilarious when they squabbled, and always refrained from taking sides. Perry resented his shaky loyalties. "Why do you care, Archie? Aren't Dio and I always frowning at each other?"

The expression on the face of her arch nemesis lightened, and he shook his head as if to clear it.

Pericles Andromeda Trenton was trouble. Trouble in the form of a shrew with a tongue so sharp it blistered whoever she turned it on. Comparing him to Wickham was only her latest jibe. She gloried in turning him upside down, like an arcane imp bent on his destruction.

But sometimes, Dio wanted to haul her over the crowded table and into his lap so he could kiss away her scowl. When she was seated across from him he forgot that the docket of petty, and not so petty, crimes he was prosecuting should be his first priority.

This was one of those times. Because she'd called him Dio. He was willing to overlook the comparison to Wickham because of it.

His nickname didn't sound the same falling from those rosebud lips. It sounded like praise. Or a plea. He wanted it to be both, and his cock turned painfully hard at the thought of what circumstances would elicit either. He wanted her to say his nickname and call him her god. He knew his desire was sacrilegious and filthy and inappropriate, but every single night he dreamt about showing her he'd prefer she used her tongue for something other than flaying him alive with its barbed edges.

He didn't purposefully frown at her. His frown just emerged of its own volition whenever she was near. Like it had been hiding in his pocket waiting for the perfect opportunity.

There wasn't much else Dio could do. What reaction was he expected to have when everything about his best friend's little sister both confounded and enthralled him?

Dio cleared his throat. "It wasn't a frown."

Perry nodded in agreement. "He's right. It wasn't a frown. It was a scowl. Almost a snarl."

"It was neither of those things," he half-heartedly protested. He was lying through his teeth. It had probably been both. Because nothing she did or said, no matter how outrageous, mitigated his fascination.

"Why were you not frowning, Mr. Squarehead?"

"Mr. Squarehead? I am not unyielding, Pericles."

She turned a laughing face to her brother. "I've rumpled him, Archie."

"Perry, leave Dio alone and sharpen your claws on someone else."

She stuck her tongue out at her brother and gave Dio a nod. "I'll give you a reprieve for now."

He dipped his head in kind and gave her a sarcastic smile. "How magnanimous of you."

The bold imp audaciously winked at him. "Magnanimous, Diogenes Maximus Castellano? Who says I've forgiven you?"

He gave her a look that said he wouldn't dream of being so presumptuous. "Oh, I know you haven't. You're merely biding your time."

"Dio, you should know by now that you'll never win against her. I know your closing arguments are supposedly things crafted of wit and elegance, but my little sister delights in finding the soft underbelly of all the males of her acquaintance - yours especially." Archie laughingly told him.

What Dio could never tell his friend was that his constant sparring with the man's younger sister made his blood run hot. Dio was the only one of his brothers who refused to let his emotions overrun his logic - except where Perry Trenton was concerned. If his brothers were present at this dinner, instead of running their import business in New York, they'd be looking on in disbelief and amusement. "I'm well aware that I am your sister's favorite target," he replied in disgruntlement.

The object of his irritation cocked her head and wagged her finger from across the table. "You shouldn't make it so easy for me to rile you."

He couldn't seem to help himself, and he wasn't inclined to explain why. Whenever one of Perry's prospective suitors was invited to the family dinner, and Dio was present, he was far more riled than he was now. He knew it was jealousy, and that the possessive streak that overwhelmed him at those dinners would not be graciously received. He hoped that the glares he threw in the direction of those hapless men were explained away as the urge to protect a girl he'd grown up with but had no designs on. "No, I shouldn't make it so easy for you to dig your claws in," he finally retorted.

"I agree. Sparring with you is so boring," she replied with a glint in her eyes.

Later that night, while they nursed bourbon before the fire, Archie launched an inquisition of sorts.

"So, Dio, what's going on between you and my termagant little sister?"

Dio swallowed the last of his drink and tipped his head back against the oversized armchair. "Damned if I know," he groused. "She seems determined to make a fool of me."

Archie gave him a look brimming with speculation. "I don't think that's it. Perry only throws punches like that when someone's gotten under her skin."

"Like a thorn," Dio clarified.

Archie shook his head. "No, not like a thorn. Like she can't stand the way they're stuck in her thoughts and she's trying to escape the reminder."

"Am I wrong in the way I approach her? Should I meet her ire, and upbraid her with insults of my own?"

"She's comfortable poking at you because she knows you won't retaliate. Maybe you should. It would serve her right."

Dio clenched his teeth. Archie could be very patronizing - and never more than when he turned his studied nonchalance on his sister. Dio understood why she railed against the restrictions placed against her gender. He understood why she'd taken over the town newspaper when the editor had retired. Because she wanted to make her mark. "I can't do that. Her words are more like an annoying buzz in my ear than a painful sting."

Archie shrugged. "Suit yourself."

Chapter Two

Every Sunday evening, after Perry had printed the weekly edition of the Willow Creek Crier on her Bullock press, she and her bosom friend Maude assembled the Ladies' Home Improvement Society pamphlets. Demand for the paper and the pamphlet was growing, and Perry was grateful she'd convinced her uncle and some of his partners to invest in a new press. She'd replaced the Koenig cylinder press with the Bullock and could now print more than five thousand copies in an hour. Now it was the curation of content, including the reporting, that took up the majority of Perry's time, not printing the finished product.

By design, the first four or five pages always held receipts for the perfect loaf of bread, or the most majestic cake, or homemade lavender soap. Those pages included tips for cleaning upholstery and new quilting and embroidery patterns. Those pages were deliberately innocuous. If the wrong audience opened the pamphlet, they were quickly bored and went no further than those first few pages.

Everything that came after the first five or so pages was the reason the society existed. To enlighten women. To provide them with the tools and knowledge they needed to understand and manage their own bodies and their own desires. Tonight, after Perry had assembled and stacked the last pamphlet, she lifted her head to find Maude studying her.

"You're very contemplative tonight," her friend commented with sparkling deep brown eyes. Perry shrugged. After Dio had departed last night, she'd felt a twinge of guilt for the way she'd goaded him. His reply to her last jab had been uncommonly bitter, and he'd had a wounded look in his eyes.

Perry was aware how juvenile her teasing was - reminiscent of the angry schoolgirl she'd once been. She wasn't being intentionally vicious- it was the resurfacing of old hurts she strove to keep buried.

No matter how many years passed, Perry couldn't erase the sting of abandonment she'd felt when Dio and her brothers left her confined to the parlor while they spent their days fishing and gamboling about.

As a member of what her mother coined the gentler sex, she'd endured sewing and deportment lessons while they went swimming and fencing and horseback riding.

She shook her head, annoyed at the maudlin nature of her thoughts. "Just wondering how our latest installment will be received," she said to Maude.

Maude's laugh was boisterous. "I've no doubt our audience will love it. They'll be scandalized by the explicit instructions on the proper administration of cunnilingus, and what they should demand of their husbands' tongues, but they'll love it."

Perry smiled. "This week's diary entry was quite educational."

"That's what I hold onto when the fear it could all come crashing down around our ears assails me. We are educating our friends and the women of this community. Showing them they deserve both pleasure and respect in the marriage bed and out of it." Maude gave a sharp nod to emphasize her declaration.

Maude's parents had married shortly after emancipation, and had instilled the belief in her that education was the key to rising above everything their family had endured.

"Many of the men we know, including our fathers and brothers, wouldn't condone what we're doing." Perry's brothers professed their open-mindedness, but she'd yet to convince them of the advantages of the suffragist movement or women's liberation of any kind. Whenever she broached the subject with her father, he gave her an indulgent smile, patted her hand, and advised she'd abandon such ridiculous notions once she accepted a suitor and held a babe in her arms.

Maude crossed her arms and peered over at her with obvious suspicion. "Are you having second thoughts? About any of it?"

Perry shook her head and sighed. "No. Merely wishing everything we did wasn't so clandestine by necessity."

"It's not just for us. It's for all the women we know. Especially the ones like Moira who are told the use of contraceptives is illegal, and that the marriage bed is their duty."

Their friend Moira, whose mother had once been a housekeeper for Perry's family, was Irish Catholic. She'd married a wastrel, borne three children, and almost lost her life bearing the fourth. When her philandering husband had been killed in a bar fight in Richmond six months ago, Perry and Maude had secretly rejoiced. Moira had recently scraped together all the savings she'd earned from her laundering business and bought a home on the edge of town. She'd turned it into a boarding house after her brothers had helped her renovate it.

"I know you're right, but you know how nosy Archie and his little posse can be. I'm worried I'll inadvertently let something slip and he'll pounce on it. What if he gets the town prosecutor involved when he tries to ferret out what I've been hiding?"

Maude tipped her head to the side and tapped her chin. "Archie wouldn't betray you like that, would he? And can't you manage the town prosecutor? You grew up with him."

Perry snorted. "Archie wouldn't expose my secrets on purpose- he'd do it in a misguided effort to protect me."

"And Mr. Castellano?" Maude asked as she crossed her arms.

"He's the opposite of manageable. He's always been that way. And we don't exactly have an affinity for one another."

"I've noticed you get very prickly when his name is mentioned."

"He's infuriating!"

"More infuriating than Archie?"

Perry frowned. "Yes. Archie might be a bumbling idiot sometimes, but he doesn't treat me like a child. Dio has this way of scowling that makes you feel duly chastened."

"You're convinced he's scowling in disapproval?"

Perry shrugged. "I can think of no other reason for his foreboding countenance where I'm concerned."

"Well, if you can't, I can. Remember I was there the day you thought Archie permanently maimed him with that wild pitch. I saw the way you dropped to your knees at his side. Even from halfway across the field I could sense the tension. I think he would have kissed you if your brothers hadn't interrupted."

Surely Maude was wrong. Perry was convinced her ridiculous fascination was one-sided. "He would never kiss me. He thinks I was set on this earth to annoy him."

"Do you want him to kiss you?"

"Ugh. No. He's as boring as the law books he used to carry around."

Maude laughed. "Then you don't find him boring at all. You love the legal aspect of your reporting. Especially if you think the trial is scandalous or prurient."

Perry wrinkled her brow. "Those aren't the sorts of books he carried around. They were all about contracts and property law. I think he became the town prosecutor because he wanted to stay close to his family."

"I think your brother's best friend has just as many secrets as you do."

****

Perry scurried through the rain, cradling the stack of pamphlets to her chest. She had fifty deliveries to her subscribers remaining. She was so intent on shielding the bundle from the light drizzle that had just begun to fall, she barreled unseeing into a solid figure that rounded the corner and strode into her path.

The man bounced back with an audible "Oof!" and nearly landed in the puddle pooling in front of the mercantile.

When he removed his hat to swat the droplets of mud from the brim, Perry groaned.

"Where are you going in such a hurry, besom?" Dio Castellano asked with a frown.

"These are the last of the pamphlets I need to distribute."

"I thought you distributed newspapers, not pamphlets." His comment was full of suspicion.

"I hand deliver the bi-monthly collection of recipes and housekeeping tips to all the women who subscribe to the Ladies' Home Improvement Society."

That was not all the pamphlets contained, but Perry would guard their contents with her life. Frustrated by the lack of guidance provided to women regarding contraception, female anatomy and female sexuality, Perry and her best friend Eliza had started the Willow Creek Ladies' Home Improvement and Enlightenment Society.

Under the guise of exchanging tips for domestic bliss, they openly discussed the things everyone around them tried to shelter them from. The latest of their education efforts was the scandalous translations. Perry had found the seemingly innocuous, plainly bound book between the volumes of Ovid and Catullus her father relegated to the top shelf of his study. As soon as she'd determined what the book contained, she immersed herself in translation.

She was delivering the second installment.

"I can't protect you if you're not truthful, Perry."

Perry shifted uncomfortably beneath his eagle-eyed gaze. She wasn't certain how she felt about his confession or why he thought he needed to protect her. "These are things the women in our community need access to."

"Recipes and housekeeping tips?" He ran his hand over his face, clearly frustrated by her explanation. And skeptical of it. "That's all those pamphlets address?"

Perry knew the longer she kept her true objectives from him, the more resources she could provide. She was intensely aware that what she was doing was a violation of the Comstock Act against the distribution of what society deemed licentious material. She was hand-delivering them in an attempt to skirt the law.

She met his gaze with a forthright one of her own. "Yes, that's all they are."

"I'm going to accept your explanation because I don't have a choice. I just hope whatever you're doing doesn't land you in my courtroom."

"It won't."

"I know you think it won't," he said as he circled her wrist to hold her there. "But don't forget. *I know you.*"

Perry wrenched away. "You think you know me, Diogenes Castellano. I'm not the same girl who followed you and Archie around like a lost lamb."

He laughed bitterly. "I'm well aware how much you've grown up, Pericles Andromeda Trenton."

Then why don't you act on that knowledge? She wanted to ask aloud. But she kept her questions to herself. Because

Dio was the last man she should be confiding her activities to.

"Then let me go about my business, Mr. Castellano."

"So it's back to Mr. Castellano, now? No more Dio? Not even a Diogenes?"

"I can't afford that level of familiarity," she said as she pulled away and clasped the bundle of translations to her chest.

"I wish you could."

"Because you want to protect me," she scoffed.

His expression was obdurate. "Yes. From yourself."

"I find it exasperating and annoying you think I'm incapable of doing that myself." He was treating her like a child, and she was most certainly not a child. She wanted him to see that. To acknowledge it. To see her. As the woman she'd become, not the girl he thought he knew.

He placed his hand on her forearm and whirled her around, so her back was pressed against the brick side of the dry goods shop and the eaves sheltered her from the rain. "You're too reckless," he insisted as he tipped her chin up with one gloved hand. "You always have been."

She set her palm in the middle of his chest, determined to push him away.

But it was the first time she'd touched him like this since he was a scrawny seventeen-year-old. He'd filled out since then. The muscles she felt shifting beneath her touch shouldn't belong to someone who wore spectacles and spent his days poring over dusty legal tomes. She wasn't going to be able to budge him. Not a single inch.

"I'm not so easily gotten rid of," he loftily informed her as he tucked a stray curl beneath her bonnet.

Perry stared into his face. Flummoxed. She needed to distract him from his questions.

That's when she noticed how impossible he found it to keep his gaze from flicking to her lips.

Perry had never been the one to initiate a kiss, but if that's what it took to distract him, that's what she would do.

She rose slightly, shifted her bundle beneath one arm, and slid the other arm around his neck. When she placed her lips against his, he exhaled, but remained still as a statue. Until Perry slicked her tongue across the bottom lip that had enthralled her for the last six years.

That stroke unleashed something in him. He lifted her more firmly against him, his hands no longer gingerly touching her waist, but firmly grasping it. "Your little ploy to distract me won't work, Pericles," he whispered into her ear.

Perry laughed throatily. "I wouldn't be so sure of that," she said as she snuck her hands into the opening of his coat and cupped his backside.

It was even more firm and delectable than the bottom lip she'd been dreaming about.

"Still not distracted, Perry," he murmured. His hands traveled the elongated contour of her ribcage. That touch belied his words.

Perry noted the hoarseness of his voice with satisfaction. Apparently, she wasn't the only one susceptible to unraveling. She bit the bow in the center of his top lip and grabbed a generous handful of arse at the same time. He balked at her touch and with a muttered curse, stepped directly between her legs.

Perry was fiercely glad bustles only adorned the backs of her gowns. Because if her dress had been cursed with a bustle in the front, she wouldn't have known exactly how much she distracted Dio Castellano.

She leaned forward and scraped her teeth along the taut cords of his neck because they were broadcasting how hard he was trying to resist her. Just like the rigidity she felt through the cotton of her skirt and petticoat.

With a groan, he finally gave in. "Everything about you is against my better judgment, Perry. Especially kissing you.."

"Just shut up and kiss me back, Dio," Perry said. And she knew the kiss was about far more than distraction.

"Archie would kill me if he knew about this, but right now I can't muster up a single damn," he grumbled before he swooped.

His hands went to her bonnet first, his body holding her fast against the wall as he loosened the knots. Just enough that it dangled down her back when he pushed it over her hair.

He took a tendril of wet hair that curled against her neck and tugged it. His eyes were glazed, and a little feral. There was no denying that Perry had broken through the impassive mask he'd leveled in response to her quips at supper.

The rain had intensified, and she felt it lashing against the back of his coat where her hands were still latched around him. He seemed oblivious to it - even as it poured from the brim of his hat in a steady stream, soaking them both.

Cold drops scattered over her bodice, his hands peculiarly warm against her chilled skin as he pushed aside the edges of her cloak. This close, the cedar notes in his cologne mingled with the scent of damp earth. The pads of his fingers were calloused where they massaged her collarbone, and his lips brushed over her chin and cheeks with a restrained fierceness she didn't recognize. As if he was afraid to fully unleash himself.

"You're procrastinating," she chided.

"Not procrastinating, savoring. Because I'll likely never get another chance."

Perry tugged impatiently on his collar and used her grip on his backside to press him closer. His tongue sank inside her mouth, brushing against her teeth and the roof of her mouth before tangling with her own. He tasted like whiskey and sunlight, and she wanted to inhale him.

His hips moved against hers as he deepened the kiss.

When he tangled his hands in her hair, his broad palms cupping her jaw, something in her chest loosened and spiraled. He tilted her face up, his kiss like that of a starving man.

The rattle of carriage wheels over the cobblestoned street jolted them from their cocoon. His hands slid away and he looked down at her, breathing heavily.

She looked back, her own lungs inexplicably burdened.

His gaze was haunted. "This cannot happen again."

Perry shoved down the prick of hurt caused by his words. "I don't intend for it to. Especially since I sufficiently distracted you," she said as she placed her hand in the middle of his chest and thrust him away.

His features hardened. "I'll go to your parents if I have to. I know whatever you're doing is unmindful of the dangers it poses."

"As I told you earlier, I'm more than capable of tending to my own affairs."

She straightened her bonnet, gave him a jaunty salute, and walked away. Leaving him standing in the rain.

Chapter Three

Dio watched her walk away and wondered what had come over him. The rain was dissipating, as if the torrent a moment ago had been nothing more than an echo of the turbulence she made him feel.

Even though he'd told her there could be no more kisses, he wanted them so much it nearly brought him to his knees. Her lips had unfurled like rose petals beneath his own. He'd tasted the honey from her tea, and the berry jam she'd likely slathered on her toast that morning. It made him smile, because she'd never been one to shy away from a liberal helping of preserves.

Dio thought back to the moment everything had changed.

He'd opened his eyes to the touch of Perry's hand on his jaw. Her expression had been tight with worry, tears bright in her hazel eyes – making them more blue than green. It was the first time she'd ever touched or looked at him with tenderness, and it had been intoxicating.

Archie and Cass had interrupted the intimate moment with howls of laughter. Perry had risen to her feet, fists braced on her hips. "The two of you!" She'd scoffed. "You're like overgrown children. What if you'd hurt him? Or affected his ability to do his job?"

Dio had winced and slowly stood. "I'm okay, Half-Pint," he'd winced again as she recoiled.

He'd forgotten how much she hated that nickname.

"Good. Maybe learn to duck out of the way when it's obvious my idiotic brother pitched a foul."

He'd watched her stalk away and spent the last six years wondering what would have happened if he hadn't let that nickname slip out.

Her brazen kiss tonight had surprised him. He was certain she was up to something, and he was certain the pamphlet he'd snuck into his pocket was at the heart of her scheming.

He shook his head to clear it and absently patted his pocket.

After Dio had hung his jacket to dry and stripped to his shirtsleeves, he sat down at his desk. He took a sip of Darjeeling for fortification and unfolded the pamphlet he'd swiped from Perry.

Apparently, the key to a perfect pie crust was lard. According to the recipe, it was superior to butter and made the end product light and flaky. The next page was all about the merits of lavender potpourri. Dio laid it on the desk and rubbed his temple. This was not like Pericles Trenton. He'd heard her scoff at domesticity on more than one occasion, and recipes for pie crust and sachets didn't explain the fear that had flashed in her eyes when he started questioning her, or the way she'd clasped the pamphlets to her heaving bosom.

Perry was one of the smartest people he knew. Which meant if she had something to hide, she'd camouflage it the best she could. He took another hearty sip of tea and flipped open the back page of the pamphlet.

"Eureka," he muttered. *Don't expect your lover to know what you want,* he read. *Men are rarely taught how to pleasure women and the church would have them believe mutual gratification has no place in the marriage bed. It's up to us to show them how we want to be touched.*

Dio thrust the paper to the center of his desk and glared at it. He did know her. She'd transformed her girlish mischief into something far more dangerous. She was embroiled in something far worse than he'd suspected. Something that would land her in prison if it was discovered. Something that would land her in his courtroom where he'd have to enforce the law against the only woman who'd ever stirred his heart.

He had to convince her of the error of her ways. He'd be waiting outside her office when she opened in the morning.

Dio had tossed and turned all night. Where had she obtained the information in those pamphlets? Was it gained through personal experience? The thought haunted him. He'd experimented at Harvard, but he was still a novice. If they'd stood in that alley much longer, she would have been forced to show him what she wanted.

He was leaning against the bricks when she strode around the corner, swinging her parasol and singing a bawdy tavern song he was sure Archie had taught her.

When she noticed him, she came to an abrupt halt and the song died in her throat. "What are you doing here?"

He glided toward her, his hands in his pockets, the brim of his hat pulled low over his eyes. "I stole one of your pamphlets while we were kissing."

"I was one pamphlet short, but I assumed I'd miscounted. You had no right," she argued.

"I had every right," he bit out. "What are you doing, Half-Pint? Do you want to end up in one of those cells?"

He jerked his thumb behind him in the direction of the jail and courthouse.

"I am arming the women of our community with the knowledge they deserve. And you know I don't like that nickname."

"You are flaunting the law. I could summon the constable and charge you right now," he said as he laid a hand on her arm.

She jerked away. "You wouldn't dare!"

"Of course I wouldn't. That's not my intent."

"Then what is your intent, Dio?" She fumed with her hands on her hips.

"My intent is to dissuade you from this foolish endeavor. You tempt the rancor and censure of the less liberal members of our community. Those who do not believe women should be entitled to the vote. Those that believe arming women with the knowledge in this pamphlet is a violation of the moral sanctity of your gender."

"All of the women who subscribe to the pamphlet attend our bi-monthly meetings and have professed their support of our mission. They are sworn to secrecy."

Dio shook his head at her obstinacy. "An oath of secrecy is no guarantee against discovery. What if one of your pamphlets falls into the wrong hands?" He stalked forward, until they were toe to toe and he could see the tiny flecks of gold around her irises. "What then Perry?"

"This is not a new endeavor, Diogenes. Maude and I have been engaged in this mission for over a year now."

"It may not be a new endeavor, Pericles, but thus far you have been lucky. It is only luck that has maintained your secret - not loyalty or skill. You endanger your future and your reputation with these actions."

Her jaw hardened and her expression turned mutinous. "I know the risks. What makes you believe I didn't assume them with my eyes wide open?"

"Perry," Dio grasped her arm and reeled her in, tipping up her chin with his free hand. "You could very well land in prison. For up to ten years. And though I respect your father, he is not an enlightened man when it comes to the rights of women. He would be completely within his rights to commit you to an asylum for what he believes are unnatural inclinations. You would be a pariah."

"Stop trying to protect me," she muttered as she tried to wriggle from his hold.

Dio wanted to shake her until her teeth rattled. "Someone needs to protect you - because you are clearly incapable of doing it yourself."

She stepped away and pointed her parasol at him. As if she was on the verge of skewering him with it. "Stay away from me, Dio. I'm no longer a helpless girl in braids following you and Archie around like a lost puppy."

Dio couldn't suppress his grin. The memories her vehement declaration conjured were too vivid. "You were never a lost puppy. More like a vengeful Fury."

Her gaze clouded. "If there's one thing I learned from my childhood, it's that I need to forge a place of my own when all the doors I want to open are locked and barred from the outside."

At times like this, the fragility she strove to batten down pierced his heart. "It wasn't an insult, Pericles. Furies are to be admired and feared as the minions of Hades and Nyx."

"I don't want fear, Dio. I want respect. The respect that I am due for my intellect and accomplishments. The respect I'm denied because of my gender. As an unmarried woman, I don't even truly own this newspaper or the building behind you. I manage it at the whims and indulgence of my father and brothers - even though it's my acumen that has made it a profitable venture."

"I respect you, Pericles," Dio soberly informed her.

"If you respected me, you wouldn't try to dissuade me from my course. Or call me by that ridiculous nickname."

"It is because I respect you that I want to discourage you from your recklessness. You are singular, Perry, and I don't want your potential thwarted by your own actions. And as for your nickname, well," he shrugged. "All I can say is that it fits you. The top of your head doesn't even reach the middle of my chest."

"Trust me, Mr. Castellano, my diminutive stature has no effect on my ability to crush your toes beneath the heel of my boot or use my parasol like one of your fencing blades."

Dio gave her a wicked grin. "Trust me, Miss Trenton, that wasn't an insult." He'd had countless dreams of what it would feel like to have her clamber him like a tree.

"If you feel inclined to watch my every move, that is your prerogative, but I have business to attend to. Will you step aside so I can go about it?"

Dio didn't want to step aside until he had her assurance she'd abandon her perilous undertaking. But he realized she was neither receptive nor amenable to his interference. So he stepped aside, doffed his hat and flourished a low bow in her direction. "Your majesty," he said before turning on his heel.

He didn't dare look over his shoulder. Just as she'd refused to do the day before when it was she who'd left him standing in the road chagrined and at a loss.

Chapter Four

PERRY WATCHED HIM DISAPPEAR around the corner with a scowl. He had no right to treat her like an infant who didn't know her own mind. Or like a creature who needed to be protected from itself. His insistence on guarding her virtue and her reputation had felt patronizing and insincere.

A half an hour later, when Maude closed the door behind her and hung her cloak and hat by the door, Perry was still fuming.

"You're frowning down at your notebook as if you bear a grudge toward it. And you've broken the lead in your pencil," Maude observed.

"Good morning to you too," Perry said in a tone heavy with sarcasm.

"What has put you in such a foul mood?"

"I've had two run-ins with Mr. Castellano in less than twenty-four hours."

Maude moved to the small woodstove and set the teapot on the hot surface. "Usually those encounters invigorate you. What has changed?"

"He interrupted my deliveries yesterday."

Maude's eyes widened as she turned back to Perry. "Does he know about the pamphlets or their contents?"

Perry groaned and bent over, so she could rest her cheek against the hard plane of her desk. "Yes. He took advantage of our mutual distraction to nab one of them from me."

"Your mutual distraction? How exactly did that happen?"

Maude wasn't exactly glowering, but she was clearly perturbed.

"He wouldn't stop with his questions. *You know what he's like.*"

"But you refused to answer them." It wasn't a question.

"I did. But he was like a hound chasing a fox. I had to turn his mind away from his quest."

"And you did that how?"

"I kissed him."

Maude laughed and her eyes twinkled. "I've seen the way he looks at you. I bet that caught him by surprise."

"It most certainly did. And me."

"You've kissed men before, Perry. We've both dissected our previous encounters ad nauseam. Why was this any different?"

"I tried to assert the upper hand. I grabbed his arse, Maude."

Her friend's eyes bulged at the confession. "You grabbed his arse?"

Perry nodded. "I don't know what came over me. But damn, I couldn't resist. It was round and firm and why does he hide it beneath that natty frock coat?"

"You shouldn't be thinking about his arse, Perry," Maude chastised with a giggle.

Perry raised her hand and leveled a glare in her friend's direction. "I know that, Maude. But I can't seem to help myself. If his reaction to my overture was any indication, he thinks about mine too."

Maude's brows flew to her hairline. "His reaction? How did he react?"

"There was no doubting the success of my ploy. He was *very distracted*."

"Then your gambit was the right choice."

Perry groaned. "Not exactly. I was distracted too. Distracted enough that he managed to steal one of the pamphlets without me even noticing."

Maude's sharp intake of breath echoed Perry's own fear. "Did he read it?"

"Of course he did. And was waiting at the door this morning to make a case for abandoning further distribution."

"Will he involve anyone else? Like the constable? Or your family?"

Perry shook her head. "I don't think so. He seems compelled to protect me against my own recklessness."

Maude cocked her head to the side. "If his motivation is protection, then you have nothing to fear. Because if he reveals our secret mission, he'll be forced to prosecute you."

"And lose his best friend in the process. Archie probably wouldn't approve of our actions either, but he'd stand by me. I'm not so sure of my parents."

"Your mother is best friends with the mayor's wife and has professed on more than one occasion that she believes a woman should leave the realm of politics in the hands of men."

Perry grimaced. "Yes. She has no desire for women's suffrage and if I depended on her to enlighten me about the intricacies of sexual congress or what to expect in the marriage bed, I'd be completely ignorant." Perry couldn't help but remember the epic battles that had ensued when her mother bade her remain indoors with an embroidery hoop rather than doing what she disdainfully called frolicking about the countryside. "According to my mother, my willfulness is the bane of her existence. She has frequently remarked that she despairs of me ever making a suitable match."

Maude nodded in commiseration. "My mother has made similar observations. But our family is much further down the rungs of the Willow Creek social ladder than yours. My mother's comments aren't as confining or desultory as the ones you are subjected to."

"My father abstains from inserting himself. Even though he's the one who encouraged me to pursue the newspaper. He told me he approved of the use of my trust to purchase it because it was a solid investment."

"What will he do if he finds out about the pamphlets?"

"I think he'd be furious. He gave me a benign pat on the hand when he found out about the Improvement Society - he said he was glad I was finally heeding the guidance my mother offered about decorum. He said he'd indulged my whims with the newspaper and knew I'd outgrow them when I became more amenable to accepting my place in life."

Maude scoffed in disbelief. "Your place in life? Did he elaborate?"

"My place in life alongside my future husband. As nothing more than a reflection of his accomplishments. As nothing more than a pale mimicry he escorts about town."

"Your father doesn't know you very well if he thinks you'll give this up in exchange for a wedding ring," she motioned around her to encompass the print shop. "You've built something he should be proud of."

"If it were Archie or Cass that had accomplished so much on their own, he'd be shouting it from the rooftops," Perry bitterly observed.

Maude frowned. "It makes no sense. Cass is out west entangled in lord knows what, and Archie is clearly miserable. You're the only one with the fortitude to create something for yourself."

Perry wanted to sigh in frustration. To vent about the reasons why she believed women had to try five times as hard to earn the recognition they deserved. But she knew her complaints were shared by her best friend, and nothing would change until their gender had an equal voice in the governance of their country.

"We must find a way to deliver the pamphlets that will escape his notice."

"If we hire a go-between or a courier, we run a greater risk of discovery. There is no anonymity in what we're doing."

"Let me think about it. There has to be a way to continue on that doesn't jeopardize what we've built. The women have confessed that the things the pamphlets have taught them have only enhanced their marital relationships, and that they no longer feel trapped by lack of knowledge or resources."

"I shall examine all the options as well. There has to be a palatable solution to our dilemma."

As Perry studied the social calendar her mother had given her yesterday, she mulled her options. Though her mother didn't like it, Perry only agreed to be trussed up for attendance at those events if she could use them as an opportunity to find stories for the paper. The spring home and garden tour was the event of the season, and Perry was resigned to making an appearance. The first stop on the tour was the mayoral residence on the outskirts of town, and a suitable gown and lavish hat had been commissioned for the occasion.

Chapter Five

Dio had kept his distance from Archie since his encounter with the man's younger sister. He hadn't wanted to avoid his best friend, but Dio didn't trust his own ability to keep his knowledge of Perry's illicit activities to himself.

When someone rapped at his front door, he set aside his tea and the tome on property law and vestiture he'd been examining. Archie stood on the threshold, brandishing a full bottle of spirits, his cheeks and eyes bright as he stamped his feet.

Dio couldn't very well leave him standing there, so he ushered him in.

"You've either been buried in work or avoiding me," Archie observed as he set the bottle on a side table and laid his coat over one of the armchairs.

"Buried," Dio agreed. There'd been a string of bank robberies in the state, and the last heist had happened in the neighboring town. The prime suspects were finally in custody and his colleague had asked him to help with the brief.

"You and Perry are too devoted to industry."

Dio schooled his features so he wouldn't betray his reaction to the casual mention of the woman he was determined to exorcise from his wayward thoughts. "She has a paper to run and I'm busy keeping Willow Creek safe from criminal elements."

"That never stopped you before. But the two of you have been absent from family dinners for at least a week." Archie narrowed his gaze suspiciously. "If I didn't know how much the two of you detested each other, I'd think you were in collusion."

He shook his head in adamant denial. "No. You know your sister and I are like fire and ice. We can hardly abide one another's presence."

Archie snorted. "You're all ice and she's all fire."

Except for when they weren't, Dio silently mused. Except when their bodies and wills were perfectly melded. As they had been in the alley when she delivered that incendiary kiss.

"She's too reckless. Why does your father permit it?"

"Permit it?" Archie gave him a look of disbelief. "There's no permitting, Dio. You are well aware of what she's like. Headstrong, stubborn and independent. It's in her very nature to be reckless and heedless of the consequences of her actions. At least the paper keeps her occupied."

Nefariously occupied. Dio sighed and ran his hands through his hair. He'd keep her secrets. He owed her that at the very least - as penance for the way he and her brothers had once excluded her. He went to the sideboard and extracted two cut crystal tumblers. "Let's drink."

Archie obliged, pouring the coffee colored whiskey into their glasses. He clinked his glass to Dio's, "Here's to friendship."

Dio nodded and drained his glass. "To friendship," he echoed.

"So does this mean you won't stay away so long next time?"

"It's only been a week. My absence was much longer while I was at Harvard."

"But that was before Cass left."

"So I'm a substitute for your older brother? I thought we were the three musketeers."

"That's not what I meant. We were. We are. But when you're there it's easier to forget it's been six months since my brother answered any of my letters."

Dio winced in sympathy and thumped his friend's shoulder. Of the three of them, Cass had always been the most aloof and resentful. "I'll make sure I'm there Tuesday evening."

Archie nodded sharply. "Good. I could use your company at the garden party tomorrow too."

Dio scraped his hand over his face again. "There was an invitation in my mailbox last week, but I was hoping I could ignore it."

"Nope. I'm recruiting you to help me keep Perry out of mischief. Our mother asked me to make sure she keeps her barrage of questions to a minimum since the governor and his wife will be in attendance."

"Why would the governor bother attending a garden party in Willow Creek?"

Archie shrugged. "He's not popular, and neither is his party."

"There's a reason for that," Dio darkly observed. "His policies aren't popular. There are those who don't want the descendants of slaves to have access to an education. I applaud what he and the Readjuster Party are trying to accomplish, but they've lost power since the incident in Danville."

Last November, just before the election and for days afterward, a racially motivated street fight had erupted into violence. Most of the residents of Danville were black, and the violence ended in the deaths of four of them. The coverage by the Richmond Dispatch placed the blame on the men who'd died, while the Willow Creek Crier had called out the supremacists. That's when Dio had finally realized Pericles Trenton was all grown-up with sentiments and aspirations that matched his own.

Dio had been proud of Perry the day she released her coverage and analysis of the events. She'd clearly seen through the rhetoric to the heart of the matter, and exposed the rot at the heart of the state's treatment of its citizens. Something he tried to do when he was asked to back up magisterial actions that were discriminatory and a misappropriation of the law. He did what he could to combat the corruption. "So Governor Cameron is attending the party because of your sister's coverage of the massacre?"

Archie raised his brows. "I hadn't thought of that. But possibly. You know the state Democratic party painted the whole incident with a tarnished brush and used it to cement their power and declare a majority. I'd forgotten Perry's editorial was supportive of the Readjuster ideals and cast blame on the white antagonizers instead of the resident blacks."

"I admired her tenacity and refusal to give an untruthful version of events that was more palatable to those in power."

Archie whistled. "Father was furious when he read it, and I swear Mother walked around tight-lipped and poker-arsed for at least two months. The article wasn't a favorable portrayal of some of Father's cronies in Richmond and he was embarrassed she'd written it without consulting him first. Mother of course thought Perry shouldn't take sides since it wasn't a genteel reflection of the delicate sensibilities of her sex. I don't know what Perry said to him in his study when he tried to reprimand her, but whatever it was, he said she'd convinced him she wasn't a muckraker and he'd allow her to follow her notions of journalistic integrity."

"She's not afraid of much, is she?" Dio asked as he poured himself another two fingers of whiskey.

Archie held out his glass for another medicinal dose. "I think the only thing my sister is afraid of is disappointing her own ambitions. And sometimes our mother."

"What's to become of the paper once she marries?" Dio's question was nothing but deliberate nonchalance.

"She'll never marry. She's said she'd rather surrender herself to the Spanish Inquisition than mortgage all her hard-won independence on the altar of matrimony."

Dio huffed in amusement. "That sounds like something she'd say."

Archie lifted his glass to the light and turned it about. "You know, I always thought the two of you would end up together."

He couldn't suppress the dread that wriggled in his stomach at his friend's words. He coughed to cover his confusion. "What would ever give you that impression? We're constantly at each other's throats."

"Dio, don't be absurd. I've noticed the way you've looked at her since the baseball game."

"That was six years ago. And you haven't mentioned it until now."

"Because she's twenty-seven and I don't know how much longer our parents will tolerate her antics. I'd rather see her settled with someone who respects her than someone who'll cage her."

"She would never have me, Archie," Dio said as he stared morosely into his empty glass.

"She might surprise you, Dio. My sister is the most prickly when her feelings are involved, and I have never seen her as prickly toward someone as she is toward you."

"I thought brothers never wanted to see their younger sisters with their friends. Isn't it a violation of some secret pact?"

"Maybe brothers who are idiots. I know you're a good man, Dio, and I know you'd protect her with your life. And I think you have feelings for her too."

"She's going to refuse me."

"Maybe you just need to ensure she sees you as someone other than who she thinks you are."

Dio glowered at his oldest friend. "What do you mean by that?"

Archie clasped his hands around his knee and gave Dio a pitying look. "Dio, you know what you're like. All you care about is the pursuit of justice."

He was stung by Archie's accusation. "That's not true. I want a family someday."

Archie leaned forward. "Then start acting like it instead of burying yourself behind your spectacles and your mountain of books. You can start by attending the garden party tomorrow."

Dio hated social situations that didn't have hiding places. And garden parties were the worst. Out in the open, with rose bushes and simpering women with fluttering lashes, a garden party was his worst nightmare.

But maybe the only way to convince Perry of the error of her ways was to do so as her husband.

"If I say yes, I'll attend, you have to promise me a bottle of whiskey to soothe my nerves when it's over."

Archie sprang up and stretched out his hand. "Done!"

Dio reluctantly shook his hand. "Since it's at the mayoral home, do I need to take my surrey? Or one of my horses? Or will I be considered gauche and inexcusable if I walk?"

"You can walk, but don't arrive looking like you walked. Leave in plenty of time so you can make the trip at a leisurely pace. My mother and her friends frown upon male exertion of any kind - especially male exertion that announces itself with damp armpits."

"I'll arrive early, then, so as not to offend."

"It's inane, I know. But if my mother had her way, all bodily functions and excretions she considers repulsive would be banished from conversation and existence."

Dio broke into laughter. "It must have been a sore trial indeed for her to raise you and Cass."

"You know it was." Archie tipped back the last dregs of his glass. "I think her censure and unyielding behavior had as much to do with Cass's departure as Father's constant needling."

"Do you think he'll ever return?"

Archie shrugged. "I don't know. I haven't heard from him in ages. I don't know whether he's dead or alive, though I assume Father is keeping tabs and would inform us if he'd met his demise."

"He used to devour the cowboy dime novels. We shouldn't have been so surprised when he caught the train to Denver."

"He escaped and left me here to fill the shoes Father was trying to make him fit into. It isn't fair."

Dio knew his friend wanted to explore the frontier too, but in a completely different way than his brother was doing it. Archie wanted to use his anthropology degree to document the culture of the native people who lived there. He'd confessed to Dio on more than one occasion that he abhorred the thought of diluting and erasing the vibrant fabric of those cultures with boarding schools and reservations. Dio agreed with him, but didn't believe Archie's father would ever allow him to pursue those passions.

"No it isn't fair. But life isn't fair. If life were fair I wouldn't be attending a garden party tomorrow," he said in an attempt to lighten the mood.

"You're right," Archie said as he straightened. "I have to have confidence it will all work out."

That wasn't exactly what Dio had meant, because in his experience, the best laid plans were always the first to go awry.

After his friend had left, Dio's dread increased, until it was a ball of lead in his gut. He was virtually certain he'd been the only one moved by the kiss he and Pericles had shared. The more he stewed over it, the more convinced he became that she would reject his suit.

But there was no help for it, because he'd just promised Archie he'd be in attendance tomorrow.

Chapter Six

PERRY STARED AT HER reflection in dismay. Her mother had insisted on decking her out in bright yellow. She looked like a garish approximation of a daffodil. Not springlike in the least. She had a hat to match. It wasn't a jaunty one like her riding hat. Instead it was a monstrosity with a brim overflowing with dried fruit and what she'd realized in disgust was a taxidermied canary. She'd bitten her tongue nearly in half so she wouldn't lose the contents of her breakfast when her mother had pinned it to her head.

Her mother's smile was like that of a cat. One who'd just devoured a bowl of cream or perhaps a canary. Maybe even the canary currently affixed to Perry's monstrous hat.

"You shall make quite the impression on the governor and his entourage," her mother assured her as she patted her arm.

Perry imagined she would. The impression an awkward, bilious, lopsided stork would make. The entire ensemble made her complexion sallow, and her eyes looked dull.

She absently wondered if Dio Castellano would be in attendance. She looked forward to sparring with him, but also dreaded him seeing her trussed up like a fatted calf.

"Perry," her mother said conspiratorially as she adjusted Perry's collar, "This is your chance to make a brilliant match with one of the young statesmen who shall be accompanying the governor and his wife. You are well past the age for settling into a comfortable marriage."

Perry knew it did her no good to protest. Her mother was of the opinion that a stable marriage could solve all the ills of the world, or ensure one turned a blind eye to them.

"I shall endeavor to appear amicable," Perry replied with a self-effacing smile that didn't reach her muddy eyes.

After the third obsequious diplomat had ogled her bosom instead of gifting her with intelligent conversation, Perry decided she needed a hiding place.

She strode into the depths of the gardens, until the murmur of the crowd had faded, and found a sturdy bench. She unpinned her hat with a sigh of relief and retrieved the flask of bourbon from her pocket.

"Care to share some of that?" A disgruntled voice said from somewhere over her shoulder.

When Perry cracked open her eyelids again, Dio Castellano was leaning casually against a tree in her line of sight. He'd hooked his suit jacket over his shoulder and his sleeves were rolled to the elbows. His hair was mussed and his spectacles were askew. As if he'd been tramping through the bramble to escape wild animals.

He looked the most relaxed she'd ever seen him, and she wondered if the bourbon would relax him into someone completely unrecognizable.

She shrugged and patted the bench beside her. "There's plenty for the two of us."

He eased himself down beside her and tilted his head back. His eyes were half-closed. "Inane conversation exhausts me," he confessed.

"I have the same complaint. I wish men would listen to my opinions instead of ogling my person."

"And I wish the unmarried women would show me who they are as a person instead of regaling me with their ability to bake an apple pie."

Perry lifted a hand to her mouth to quell the laughter tickling her throat. "I shouldn't find your plight hilarious, but I can't help but wonder how you'd react if one of them broached one of the more salacious topics covered in the pamphlets."

"I'd probably be tongue-tied. But at least it would be more interesting than a discussion of the most efficient way to core an apple."

Perry giggled and handed him the flask. "For each swig we'll divulge one thing we'd rather discuss than coring apples."

He took a swig and she had to look away from the sinuous bob of his throat. "I'd much rather discuss how much I detest corsets."

That wasn't the sort of revelation she'd been expecting. "I know why I detest them, but why do you detest them, Mr. Castellano?"

His gaze glimmered with a hint of naughtiness. "They impede one's view. I'd much rather see the outline of how a woman is truly formed."

"They also impede one's breathing. And can cause very serious health issues - including impacted lungs and menstrual anomalies."

"I have read of these impacts as well. Just more strikes in the column against their use."

He handed the flask back to her.

Perry took a swig and considered what to say. "I wish I could talk about the suffrage movement instead of coring apples."

"I don't think the governor would be averse to hearing it - just not from the lips of a woman."

"Yes. Because we're still seen as mentally inferior or morally dependent by most of the country."

He extracted the flask from her loosened grip, his fingers brushing against hers. Perry felt the tingle all the way to her elbow. "Shall we talk about suffrage, Perry?"

"I'd like that. There's no one I can discuss personal liberties with besides Maude."

He took another sip from the flask and proffered it to her again. "What sorts of personal liberties would you like to discuss?"

She twisted in her seat so she was facing him. "Can you explain why sexual experimentation has a double standard?"

"Easily. Because motherhood is never in doubt, but fatherhood is. Unless a man can be certain there's an impregnable fortress around the object of his affection."

"So men view sexual congress as nothing more than a means of securing progeny?"

He shook his head. "No. Sexual congress with a woman a man deems respectable is for securing progeny. Sexual congress with a woman who lacks what society deems moral rectitude happens for a different reason altogether."

Perry nodded. "Objectively, I know this. It's the reason there's a house with a red door on the other side of the railroad tracks."

"I'm not surprised you know of places like that, despite your mother's efforts to pretend they don't exist."

Perry narrowed her gaze. "They exist because women have very few choices if they find themselves vulnerable to exploitation."

"Sometimes a woman's body is the only commodity she has."

"Which is why the pamphlets are so necessary. Yes, they show women how to celebrate their sexuality. But they also tell her how to avoid the repercussions of doing so if she would like to indulge her desires outside the structure of marriage."

"Sometimes married women become tired of childbearing as well. Though I don't doubt my mother's love, at times I wonder if she would have given birth to twelve children if she'd had any choice in the matter."

"You should ask her."

His smile was swift. "I wouldn't dare. She'd think I was criticizing her in some way."

Perry returned his smile. "Or she'd come after you with her rolling pin."

"That too," he agreed.

"We've consumed half the flask. I think that's more than enough fortitude to endure the lackluster conversation that awaits us."

He lifted his watch from his waistcoat and peered at the face. "It's nearly four o' clock. The invitation stated the party would end at half-past. We only have to bear another thirty minutes."

"Will you help me pin my hat back on?"

He picked it up and gave her a look of horror. "Is that an actual dead canary?"

Perry covered her eyes and groaned. "I think so. It's horrific, isn't it?"

"I don't think I possess the vocabulary to express my abject terror."

"Neither do I. And you're a prosecutor and I'm an editor - so that alone speaks to how ghastly it is."

"I assume it wasn't your choice?"

"No. I'd ask you to close your eyes, but then you'd likely stick us both with the pins."

"I'll endeavor not to look at it," he reassured her.

Chapter Seven

Dio gingerly set the hat atop her head. Her coiffure was still mostly intact, and as much as he was tempted to tuck the tendrils that had escaped back into her low chignon, such a choice would be hazardous. The faint scent of summer roses clung to her skin, and his thumb swept through the sheen of perspiration pooled at her nape. He wanted to bend low and sink his nose and teeth there. He knew this respite presented him with a golden opportunity to propose, but the words stuck in his throat.

"There," he said as he slid the last pin behind her ear. "Shall we return?"

He stood and pitched his elbow toward her.

She stood as well, and after she brushed off her skirts, she slipped her hand in the crook of his arm. "We shall," she said as she defiantly tipped her chin. She looked like an empress - imperial and remote. Nothing like the giggling woman who'd handed him a flask of bourbon and shuddered at the nightmare of her haberdashery moments ago.

Dio led her to the gaggle of women surrounding her mother. When they'd taken a place at the edge of the circle, Agatha Trenton's gaze strayed to the place Perry's hand rested.

She'd kept her hand in the crook of his arm, and her fingers were clenched tightly against his skin. As if she was pulling strength from him.

Her mother's gaze strayed there, lingered, and speared him with a sharp look he couldn't decipher.

"Pericles, have you made the acquaintance of young Mister Fortenham?"

The question was Mrs. Trenton's refusal to acknowledge his presence at her daughter's side. He'd been assessed and found lacking. The curt dismissal made his jaw tighten in anger. As if Perry sensed his reaction, she smoothed her fingers over the skin of his inner elbow. Soothing him.

"Yes, Mother. Mister Fortenham and I exchanged pleasantries earlier this afternoon. He informed me that he is an avid devotee of lawn tennis."

Agatha Trenton nodded as if she approved of such a ridiculous obsession.

"I am one of the founding members of the National Lawn Tennis Association," the man said as he puffed out his chest.

Out of the corner of his eye, Dio saw Perry bite her lip. As if she was curbing her laughter at his pomposity. He knew she could feel the shiver of his muscles beneath her touch and hoped she was aware he was fighting back an inappropriate reaction as well.

"An admirable feat," his companion managed to eke out.

"Mrs. Trenton, I promised your daughter some refreshment and would be remiss if I didn't fulfill my duty. May we be excused?"

Dio wondered if Perry had noticed her mother's very purposeful snub of his presence, and if she would be grateful for his intervention so she could finally laugh.

"We wouldn't want her to wilt any further because she was famished," her mother caustically replied.

The temperature was uncharacteristically sweltering for late April, and apparently Perry's foray into the garden had affected her appearance.

When they were out of sight, they sighed in unison. "Thank you for engineering our escape," Perry said as she squeezed his forearm.

"I think she was scandalized by my rolled sleeves and wrinkled jacket." The thought delighted Dio.

"It may be some time before you receive another invitation to dine with us."

"Archie issued me a standing invitation - for whenever I need to escape the chaos of my own family or the solitude of my bachelor quarters."

"I wish I had a standing invitation to go somewhere else," she grumbled.

Dio's arm tensed beneath her grasp. "You're always welcome to dinner with my family. If you don't mind shouting and wrestling across your dinner table."

"I'd much rather have that than the cold silence my mother prefers. Your attendance is a welcome distraction and you're sorely missed when you stay away."

He noted her blush and surmised she was aware her comment could be construed as a confession that she missed him.

"If I'm absent too long, I sorely miss trading insults with you," he said as he gave her hand a light squeeze.

"So this solidarity of purpose isn't a permanent condition?"

He chuckled. "According to Archie we're like fire and ice. I've no doubt we'll be at each other's throats again soon."

"Perhaps I'll refrain. You make quite the knight in shining armor," she confided.

"I think you'd be grateful to anyone who removed you from your mother's draconian clutches - even poor Fortenham."

Her nose wrinkled in distaste. "You're a much better option than Fortenham."

"I choose to interpret that as grudging flattery."

"Suit yourself," she said with a graceful nod and a mischievous wink.

After he'd secured two lemonades and a slice of white cake garnished with strawberries, he led her to a table beneath one of the tents.

She leaned over once they were seated. "I declined a slice of cake in case my mother was watching, but I wouldn't mind a taste of yours," she wheedled.

Dio lifted a forkful of fluffy cake and strawberries toward her. "Be my guest," he said as he cupped his hand beneath it. "But you have to tell me why a slice of cake would earn you a scolding."

Her mouth enveloped the tines of the fork, and she snuck out her tongue to clean the strawberry residue she'd missed. After her obvious savoring had made Dio harder than he'd thought possible, she reclined and clasped her hands over her midsection. "My mother doesn't approve of my hips."

"There's nothing wrong with your hips."

"According to my mother, they are too wide for current fashion."

Dio scoffed. "Men love hips like yours. Your mother is a fool."

"Men like you, Dio?"

He dipped his head in acknowledgment.

She braced her elbows on the table. "Why?"

"We're not having this conversation."

Her giggle filled the space between them. "I like making you squirm, Dio Castellano."

"Why are the two of you ensconced over here in the shadows?" Archie's bright voice interrupted their locked gazes.

"We're trying to stay out of Mother's orbit," Perry explained.

Archie pulled out the remaining chair at their table and collapsed into it with a heave of relief. "A wise decision. I believe I shall join you."

"I thought you were the golden child. You should have no reason to hide," Dio said.

Archie's answering grin was rueful. "No such luck, old chap. I may be the apple of Father's eye right now because I've agreed to learn the ropes of the family business, but there is no pleasing Mother. No matter how sprightly I dance attendance."

"I've concluded she thinks we're all her little marionettes and she's happiest when she's pulling our strings," Perry bitterly muttered.

"Weren't you going to interview the governor and his party for the paper?" Archie asked.

"She was instructed to be on her best behavior."

Dio's answer made Archie turn to his sister in disbelief. "But it's your vocation. What better place to do what you do best? Pry into other people's business?"

Perry smacked her brother on the arm. "I shall have to do it unobtrusively when she's otherwise occupied."

Archie set his elbows on the table. "Sister, I'd wager your paper's defense of the governor is the only reason he deigned to attend this garden party. You have every right to introduce yourself and pursue that connection."

Dio touched her arm, and when her eyes met his he saw a flicker of uncertainty in their depths. "Archie has the right of it. Don't let your mother intimidate you today."

She took a deep breath and tightened her jaw. "You're both right. I refuse to be a marionette today." She stood and shook her skirts out.

"You're doing it now?" Archie asked.

"There's no better time than now," she resolutely replied over her shoulder as she glided away.

After she was out of range, Archie quirked a brow at Dio. "So I take it you didn't broach the subject of a union between the two of you?"

Dio shook his head. "The right moment never seemed to present itself."

"My sister isn't one for perfumed bouquets and florid sentiment. You could have asked her in simple terms - offered it as a solution to her dilemma."

"How do you know she isn't one for flowers and sentiments?"

Archie scoffed. "Because I do. Those things don't appeal to her."

Dio suspected Archie was wrong but didn't want to openly contradict him. "Then I won't ply her with them. Instead, I'll take her aside at dinner on Tuesday and plead my case."

Archie beamed. "Capital! There's no reason she should refuse."

There were thousands of reasons she could refuse him, but Dio hoped she agreed.

Chapter Eight

Perry braced herself as she strode toward the cluster of guests gathered around the governor and his wife. "Governor, I'd like a word when you have the chance. I'd like to chronicle your thoughts about the political climate in our state for the Willow Creek Crier."

The governor's expression lightened at her proposal. "Ah. Miss Trenton. We are grateful for your support of our causes," he sketched a miniature bow in her direction.

Perry thought it a trifle imperious that he referred to himself in the third person, but extended a curtsey in return.

"I shall make my excuses," he told his entourage. "Come, Miss Trenton. I am eager to speak with you."

Once they were seated, Perry posed her first question. "Governor, my readers are interested to hear what additional reforms your administration will be promulgating.

The end of the poll tax, the equal pay requirement for teachers regardless of race, and the establishment of the Virginia Normal and Industrial School and Longwood University are just some of the steps you've taken to better serve all the citizens of the state."

"Have you heard, Miss Trenton, that we are in the process of building Virginia's first mental asylum for black citizens?"

"I haven't heard of this initiative and will make certain I highlight it in my article. I'd like to hear your thoughts on the Danville Circular and its blatantly discriminatory statements, and how you believe it led to the riot."

Governor Cameron signaled one of the servers for a glass before giving Perry his full attention. Once he'd taken a sip of lemonade, he replied. "The circular spread scurrilous lies about the Negro judges my administration had appointed and the leasing of stalls in the city market to Negro merchants. The appointment of those qualified individuals, and the increased commerce and economic advantage of those merchants, cannot be underscored. The members of the opposition party had become comfortable holding these advantages only for themselves, and indulged in fear mongering that led to the deaths of five Danville citizens."

"Other sources have told me they believe the Funders want to implement structural changes that will protect their power."

"For reasons you can well imagine, Miss Trenton, the multi-racial composition of the Readjuster party threatens the status quo these men have become accustomed to. They suffer under the misapprehension that anyone else given a seat at the table is consuming their meal. They don't realize the meal is a banquet much like that of the fishes and loaves, and there is plenty to go around."

"Governor, I'd be honored if you'd share your thoughts on the Women's Suffrage movement here in Virginia."

"As you know Miss Trenton, Miss Langhorne's attempt to vote in the last presidential election was unsuccessful. And the Virginia State Woman Suffrage Association is on the wane and balancing on the edge of fading into obscurity. Although my party favors education for women, I do not believe the time is yet ripe to give women the vote."

"Thank you for your candor, sir," Perry said.

"Miss Trenton, may I be frank?"

"Please. I would appreciate it."

"It is the general feeling of myself and most of my colleagues that a woman's place in society is nurturing future generations and serving as a bastion of morality. When women are fulfilling their Christian duty, the economy flourishes."

Perry did not agree with his sentiments, and knew those like her and Moira, who owned property and increased commerce, deserved the right to choose their elected officials. But Perry also knew that expressing her dissent would not advance her cause and would hinder it instead of helping it.

"You and my mother share common ground in your views on the subject," Perry informed him.

His eyes crinkled with amusement. "But you do not and you choose diplomacy over advocacy."

Perry stiffened. "In this instance, yes. It would not serve me to push for my cause when the audience is unreceptive."

He raised a brow at her sharp retort. "It is not that I am unreceptive, Miss Trenton. It is that society is unreceptive and any efforts to sway it will result in failure. I believe a time will come for such advocacy that will bear fruit. Remember that patience often wins where passion cannot."

Perry felt vaguely patronized, but knew she'd glean nothing more from interviewing him. "May I quote you directly, Governor?"

"So long as you don't share my views on women's suffrage, yes, you may."

She stood and offered her hand in parting. "I wish you and your party the best in the upcoming election."

He shook her hand firmly. "Your wishes are appreciated, Miss Trenton."

As Perry walked away, she knew she'd soon face her mother's wrath. Agatha Trenton would not be happy that Perry had monopolized so much of her guest of honor's precious time. Perry had been truthful about her mother's vision of womanhood, and she balked at the idea of being rendered virtually invisible.

The carriage ride back to their home was fraught with tension. Her mother finally broke the silence. "Pericles, I have tolerated Mr. Castellano as a friend of your brothers, but I will not accept him as one of your suitors. This frivolous flirtation you indulge in whenever he is near is unbecoming."

"He is not one of my suitors, Mother. But if he were, why are you so opposed? He is a man of both means and standing in our community."

"I am opposed because his family worships the pope. I'll not tolerate the presence of continental Papists in our family."

"Mother, that's abominable," Archie remarks. "Catholicism is the foundation for your Protestant beliefs."

Perry glared at her too. "You sound like one of Henry the Eighth's courtiers."

She sniffed and looked out the window. "I'll never entertain the notion of a man like that as a son-in-law."

Perry gritted her teeth in frustration. "Mother, I'll say it again and hope my declaration sinks in. Dio is not courting me. We are simply friends."

Her mother swiveled her head and peered at her. "Friends don't disappear into the shrubbery with each other."

"We didn't disappear together," Perry protested. "Dio was already there and I was looking for a place to catch my breath."

"And take a swig of your flask," Archie quipped with a grin.

Perry threw him a look that promised retribution for his betrayal.

"Were you consuming spirits at the garden party, Pericles?"

Perry probably shouldn't be deriving so much delight from her mother's horrified expression. "Only a nip, mother," she assured her with an unrepentant smile.

Agatha Trenton threw her hands in the air. "I despair of you ever behaving with proper decorum or displaying the feminine sensibilities I've tried to make you learn."

"Mother, as I've said a thousand times, the world is changing. I am not ashamed of my femininity. Nor am I ashamed to wield it when it suits me. But I refuse to be defined by it."

"Your father has been far too lenient and indulgent where you're concerned. Especially in regards to that newspaper," her mother said in distaste.

"The newspaper means I have some measure of independence and don't have to run to my father for pin money. I pay my own expenses. For instance, if it had been up to me, I would have garbed myself in something far less garish than this gown."

Her mother sneered. "If I'd left the decision to you, you would have shown up in one of those scandalous divided skirts."

Perry shrugged. "They offer ease of movement. I would eschew petticoats and bustles permanently if I didn't think it would ostracize my business."

"It's unseemly how much time you spend embroiled in your business. I despair of ever holding my grandchildren in my arms."

Archie and Perry both rolled their eyes at their mother's histrionics.

"Cass and I are also equipped to provide you with grandchildren, Mother."

Their mother turned a gimlet eye on her brother. "I've yet to witness you dance with any girl more than once, and I've never heard of you walking out. You are just as opposed to marriage as your sister."

"No, mother, I'm not. But like Perry, I too refuse to be pressured into a relationship that isn't built on mutual adoration and respect."

She flicked her gaze between the two of them in patent disbelief. "Have my children learned nothing? Respect and adoration? What about safety and security? Those are more important than some pipe dream of love."

Perry reached for her mother's hand, but she snatched it out of reach. This was how these conversations always went. Their mother was entirely unwilling to consider the merit of any viewpoint other than her own.

"Mother, we don't want the kind of marriage you and father have. You both approach it as a duty, not a joy. I'd be surprised if you've exchanged more than a handful of words in the thirty-five years you've been united."

"I'll have you know that your father rules his sphere and leaves me to rule mine. My sphere ensures he is comfortable and has a haven to retire to after he's spent the day ensnared by commerce."

"You'll never see me as more than a commodity, will you?" Perry quietly asked as the hurt bloomed somewhere in the vicinity of her heart. Her mother's continuous rejection lodged there like a poisonous dart.

"If I've taught you nothing else, remember this, daughter. In this world, women are nothing more than a commodity to be bartered and sold. Our value lies in our capacity to bear children and our ability to provide ease."

Perry had known her mother harbored anti-suffragist beliefs, but she'd never observed such a vehement response. "If that's all you believe women are good for, I pity you, Mother."

"It is I who should pity you, Daughter. Your rebellious leanings will either land you in prison or ensure you die alone."

Archie whistled. "Harsh, Mother."

"You're no better, Son. Your reluctant embrace of the family business because you'd rather be studying shards of pottery and rain dances is just as unbecoming and shameful as your sister's proclivities."

Archie shook his head. "You may pity us, but I pity Father. You're relentless. And so blind to the wonder of the world around you. The things I've studied are far more than shards of pottery."

Their mother huffed and pointedly ignored them for the rest of the journey.

After their mother had retired, Perry found Archie on the back porch. "I miss him, Archie." She said as she plopped into the porch swing beside her brother.

Archie took a long drag on his cigar and rested his head against the back of the swing. "I do too," he admitted. "I don't want to follow in our father's footsteps."

"But Cass is out west following his dreams because he couldn't stand what was being asked of him."

Perry knew Archie couldn't stand it either. But he felt like he had no choice in the matter.

"And I'm stuck here. When all I want is to go west and document a way of life that's becoming extinct," her brother continued.

Archie's studies were important to him. He truly cared about the encroachment of civilization on the indigenous way of life. He wanted to be in the field, using his anthropology degree to explore and highlight the culture and stories that were disappearing, "Do you think he'll come home if Father insists?"

Archie shook his head. "No. Not unless Father gives Cass no choice. Not unless I leave and there's no other choice."

"Are you leaving, Archie?"

He shrugged. "I've had offers and I've wanted to take advantage of them. But Father needs me."

Perry laid her hand on his arm. "I know you love us, and you feel you're obligated to stay. Because Cass thumbed his nose at his responsibility as the oldest. But you shouldn't sacrifice your own chance at happiness and fulfillment."

"I don't think Father cares about my happiness. He doesn't understand why I pursued my studies in anthropology, and he wouldn't condone me hieing off to the back of beyond to demonstrate why they were useful." "If you could go anywhere, where would you go?"

His expression was suddenly both earnest and fierce. "Minnesota or Wisconsin."

"Why would you go there?"

"The resiliency of the Anishinabe culture is something I want to study."

"The only way he'll let you go is if Cass comes back."

Archie laughed bitterly. "He left because he wanted to escape. Because it was too much for him. You know he's brilliant - but father never understood why he gave up."

Perry's sad expression reflected his. "Cass said no matter what he did, the words were a jumble- that it was only numbers that made sense to him."

"And then father caught him kissing Moira," Archie said with a sigh.

"It was bound to end in disaster and disappointment," Perry concluded.

"There's no hope for it," Archie said morosely. "He's never coming home. I wouldn't if I was in his shoes."

Perry wrapped his hand in hers. "I think you should write to him. I think you should tell him about your dreams and ask him to come home."

"Cass and father can't get along, Perry. He was right to leave. I'm not selfish enough to make him come back."

Well, I am, Perry mused to herself. She would write Cass a letter on Archie's behalf. Wasn't meddling the primary responsibility of younger sisters?

Chapter Nine

DIO HAD NEVER DRESSED formally for a dinner with the Trentons, but something about the situation warranted it. He was going to propose to Pericles tonight.

He'd decided not to listen to Archie and the speech he'd composed wouldn't be delivered like he was negotiating a business deal. He wanted her to know that he genuinely liked her and that he thought their former animosity meant their union would be anything but boring. He was going to let her know how attracted to her he was - and that he'd been fighting his attraction for the last six years.

He'd even purchased a bouquet and a ring of peridot and onyx.

Archie's eyes went wide when he saw the bouquet. "Is that for my sister?"

Dio nodded, unable to speak past the lump of dread stuck in his throat.

"I'll get her. You don't want our mother to see you with that. Go wait on the back porch and I'll send her out."

And then his friend shut the door in his face.

Dio loosened his collar and smoothed back the cowlick draped over his cheek. His glasses were covered in condensation from the humidity, and as soon as he reached the porch he untucked his shirt so he could clean them.

He was still wiping them when the door banged against its frame. "What's so important you had to speak to me in secret? Did someone else find out about the pamphlets?"

Dio shook his head and cleared his throat. Her cheeks were flushed, the freckles across her nose as bright as copper pennies. Her mouth was slightly parted and though her eyes flashed with irritation, he wanted to kiss her.

He cleared his throat and swiped the bouquet from the railing. "These are for you," he said abruptly as he dropped to one knee.

Her gaze narrowed. "What are you doing, Dio?" She hissed.

"Pericles Andromeda Trenton, would you do me the honor of becoming my wife?"

Her reaction wasn't the one he'd expected. She put her hand beneath his elbow to jerk him upright. "No. I won't marry you Dio. You know I don't want to give up my freedom, and if I ever consider it, I will only surrender my will to someone who loves me unreservedly."

Now Dio was angry as well as embarrassed. "How do you know I don't love you?"

She smacked him in the chest with the bouquet. "I know you don't love me because we loved nothing better than insulting each other three weeks ago."

He took her free hand in his own and cradled it - even when she tried to wrench away. "Listen to me, Perry," he told her sternly.

"Fine," she said as she rolled her eyes again.

"We've known each other our whole lives. You might be my best friend's little sister, but I consider you a friend as well. As more than a friend. I'm not constantly squashing down the urge to silence Archie with kisses. I can protect you - no matter what happens."

She regarded him with suspicion. "What do you think is going to happen? Do you know something you're not telling me, Dio?"

He pushed her hand over her head, and pressed a brief kiss to the corner of her open mouth. "It's only a matter of time before you're discovered, Perry."

She wriggled her hand in his grasp, but he wasn't letting her go until she comprehended the gravity of her situation. "If something happens, I can keep you out of jail, Perry."

Her eyes were sparking fire. "Nothing's going to happen, Dio. If you're proposing marriage so you can protect me, it's wasted effort."

"My misplaced loyalty isn't the only reason I'm proposing."

"Then tell me the other reasons," she warily said.

"Sunday, when we were sitting on the bench, I admit I wanted a taste of your bourbon. But not from your flask. From your lips. And when you asked me to pin your ridiculous hat back on, I wanted to press a kiss to your nape and let your scent rest in my lungs."

He heard her gasp, and he didn't think it was a gasp of revulsion or outrage. He walked her backward and she went willingly, her eyes wide and searching.

When her back thumped against the door, he rubbed his thumb across her blooming cheek and kissed her.

This wasn't a closed mouth kiss. Because he was trying to convince her to take a chance on him. On them and what they could become. "There are many things in this life I'm uncertain of, Perry, but you are not one of them," he confessed before he swallowed another one of her tiny gasps and stroked her tongue with his.

Her free arm curled around his neck, and she draped the other one over his shoulder. She didn't drop the flowers, and that made him smile into the kiss. The fact she was still holding them meant that he'd been right and Archie had been wrong. His inclination to approach her with sentimentality wasn't being rebuffed.

As her fingers latched onto the muscle of his shoulder, she rose to her toes and aligned her body with his. Dio could feel the tickle of the ferns from the bouquet against the side of his neck, and the heady scent of roses was almost overwhelming. She smelled of roses too, but not plush, brazen red roses. She smelled of delicate wild roses, because those had more thorns than their domesticated cousins. Just as she did.

She tasted like honey and strong tea, and a hint of bourbon.

He drew back. "Pericles Trenton, do you lace your afternoon tea with spirits?"

Her grin was somehow both sheepish and devilish. "Sometimes. When mother is being more insufferable than normal."

"Have I convinced you of my sincerity?"

She sighed. "I'm not such a hypocrite that I'm afraid to admit I like kissing you. But expert kissing isn't enough to persuade me to the altar."

"Expert kissing? I'm flattered."

Her hand tightened around his neck, and Dio could feel the bite of her nails through his jacket, waistcoat and shirt. "Kissing takes practice, and it's clear you've had plenty of opportunity to perfect your craft."

"Not as many opportunities as you'd think," he told her.

"I wouldn't mind more kissing," she said as she fluttered her lashes and snuggled against his chest. "But I'm not marrying you."

Dio lifted her arms from their perch around his neck and stepped away. "It might be old-fashioned and out of synchrony with your suffragette sympathies, but I'm not going to risk destroying your reputation."

"Now who's being a hypocrite?" She scoffed. "You had no such misgivings when you backed me into an alley and kissed me within an inch of my life for the whole world to see."

"The streets were deserted and you're the one who kissed me first. You can't pick and choose when you're going to blame me for whatever this thing is that's happening between us."

She tossed her head, dismissing him. "There's nothing happening between us. There never has been."

He watched her flounce away and made his way to the front entrance again with resignation and anger. Archie answered his knock like he'd been standing there waiting.

He stepped back when he saw Dio's thunderous expression. "I can see from your face that it didn't go well. Where are the flowers? I should probably get rid of them."

"She kept them."

Archie ignored Dio's sullen tone as he rubbed his hands together and laughed maniacally. "Then she's not as averse to your suit as you think. Otherwise she would have thrown them back in your face."

Dio lifted a shoulder, at a loss to understand the man's sister. "Maybe she just liked the fact someone finally gave her some."

"Other men have tried to give her flowers, Dio. And she always tosses them back in disdain. But she didn't do it this time. I think you have a chance at winning her."

Dio sighed and ran his hands over the bristle of his jaw. He wished he'd thought to shave. His jaw was always shadowed by five o'clock in the evening. "I thought it would be easy to persuade her marriage to me was a capital idea."

"That is one part of my sister that's like our mother. She's obstinate to a fault and won't give in easily - especially if she thinks doing so would compromise her principles. Come on, you can flirt with her across the supper table."

A pair of raised voices echoed in the hallway as they neared the dining room. "If he has no designs on you, why would he bother to bring you flowers? Mr. Castellano does not seem like the type of man who would indulge in empty gestures."

"I told you mother, they are just a symbol of our friendship."

Mrs. Trenton harrumphed at her daughter's lackluster explanation. "You are either dissembling or abysmally naive, Pericles. I care not which. I'll just ask that you refrain from further shenanigans."

As he rolled the ring he'd gotten around and around in his pocket, Dio could just imagine the way the woman was shaking her finger at Perry.

Archie cleared his throat to announce their presence and both women met it with a frown. Dio didn't think his odds of persuading Perry to accept his suit would be favorable. No matter how charming he was over mounds of mashed potatoes and roast beef.

When they were all seated, Mrs. Trenton brought up the next social event she had planned. "I hope all of you will be in attendance for the town's first annual ice cream social."

"My brothers are providing the flavoring from one of the chocolatiers they befriended in New York City, and my mother has already informed me I'll be responsible for some of the cranking," Dio said to the table at large.

"I've never had chocolate flavored ice cream," Perry brightly replied. She seemed completely unaffected by what had transpired between them earlier and Dio resented her cavalier attitude. His trousers were still uncomfortably tight.

Now that he'd tasted her kiss, watching her slip her spoon into her mouth, and dab at the drop that clung to her bottom lip, was the most tortuous and erotic thing he'd ever experienced.

The conversation around him was evaluating the merits of vanilla and strawberry flavoring versus chocolate. He would have gladly defended the superiority of chocolate, but he was too distracted to follow the thread of the argument.

When the housekeeper reached for his plate, he realized it was untouched. He was inspired by the syllabub now in front of him to issue his own form of temptation. He'd noticed how her gaze strayed to his lips, so when he raised the lemon-infused dessert to his mouth, he laved the spoon, curling his tongue around it, imagining it was one of her pert breasts instead.

He kept his eyes on hers as he scooped up more dessert. Not to be outdone, she waved her own spoon in the air with a smirk.

When she inserted the bowl of the spoon in her mouth and let it rest against the inner curve of her cheek before slowly extracting it, making sure her teeth scraped the handle as she did so, he nearly surged across the table.

"Stop fucking my little sister with your eyes," Archie hissed at his side. "I'm usually oblivious to her antics, but if I noticed, Mother will notice soon."

Dio shook his head to clear it and pushed himself away from the table. "I have some briefs to finish, but I will pay my respects at the social tomorrow."

Chapter Ten

This time, Perry had insisted on choosing her own ensemble. She wore a pale green calico with mother of pearl buttons and dark green piping, and her hat was straw with a sprig of matching flowers affixed to the black band.

When Dio had informed them at dinner yesterday that he'd be in attendance, her heart had filled with trepidation. She knew refusing him had been the right thing to do, but the wounded look in his eyes when she'd rebuffed him after their kiss had haunted her dreams.

She would gladly skip this outing if she could, but she knew Maude would be there. Because they lived on opposite sides of town they rarely had the opportunity to socialize outside of the paper. Her friend lived in a vibrant community, and since her father presided over the African

Methodist Episcopalian congregation, almost all of her spare time was eclipsed with charitable missions.

Perry had never been to her friend's home, but she was determined to rectify that. The way Maude spoke of her parents was both reverent and amused, and Perry wanted to see how a parental relationship like that looked. One not burdened with disappointment and unmet expectations, but instead characterized by pride and a celebration of learning.

Their carriage was one of the last ones to arrive in the village park on the outskirts of town, and Perry held her hat steady while she scanned the crowd for Maude or Dio.

She spotted her friend with a group of women near a table laden with pies. Perry was more than partial to cherry, and she hoped it was among the offerings. The wind gusted through the trees and sent everything not held down tumbling across the bright green expanse of grass.

The way the children chased after the wheeling hats and linens with mirthful abandon made Perry smile.

Maude noticed her as she drew closer, and enveloped her in a hug. "I'm so glad you're here. Please rescue me," she murmured into Perry's ear.

She linked her arm with that of her friend. "Maude and I have newspaper business to discuss. I promise we'll return later."

When they were out of sight, Maude pulled Perry behind a tree and collapsed against its sturdy trunk. "Lord spare me from match-making mamas," she beseeched with a glance toward the heavens.

"Is that who had you cornered?"

Maude groaned. "Yes. As the last unwed daughter of Reverend Latimer, I am much sought after by women who think saddling me with their sons will raise their esteem in the eyes of the church."

"So you need to stay out of their sight for a while?"

"Please," Maude pleaded as she slumped to the ground. "Can you snag me some lemonade and something to eat? I'll have it here."

"Of course," Perry told her. "I'll be right back. Watch out for the snakes and mosquitoes."

"Ha ha," her friend retorted.

Perry poured her friend some lemonade and put a piece of roast chicken and a glob of German potato salad on a plate. She was making her way back to the copse of trees when she spied Dio.

His shirtsleeves were rolled up again, and he was crouching in front of the ice cream maker, cranking it for all he was worth.

The repetitive action pulled the cotton of his shirt taut against his back, and his buttocks flexed against the thick material of his trousers. Perry snapped her jaw back into place and turned back around. Even after she'd delivered the food to Maude, she couldn't erase the tantalizing vision he'd presented.

She reclined beside her friend and grabbed a fallen branch to fan her face and neck.

"Why are you so flushed?" Maude asked after she daintily wiped the grease from the corners of her mouth.

"Dio was taking his turn at the ice cream maker."

"Ooh.." her friend dreamily said.

"Ooh? What kind of noise is that?"

"It's one of sympathy. I'd be flushed too if I was blessed enough to find that man kneeling."

"He wasn't kneeling, he was crouching."

Maude pursed her lips and whistled. "Even better. If he'd been kneeling you wouldn't have been able to tell me what his arse looks like. I don't think he ever removes his frock coat."

Perry closed her eyes. "There's nothing that could make me forget what it looks like. I wouldn't have minded taking a bite out of it."

Maude burst into laughter. "Now that would have sent you straight to the front of the congregation to repent your sins."

"He asked me to marry him before dinner on Tuesday."

"I don't see a ring. Does that mean you refused him?"

"I had to, Maude. He doesn't love me. And I'm not surrendering my independence to a man."

"Not all men are like that, Perry. Some men encourage their wives to work and support them when they do. I think Mr. Castellano would be that sort of husband."

Perry frowned. "I can't risk losing the paper."

"Maybe he'd be willing to sign a prenuptial agreement?"

"I thought only men could require those."

Maude shrugged. "Technically, they can. But I've been reading up on contract law and I think if you made your future husband sign something that stated the paper stayed with you and then he reneged on it, the court might grant you damages and restitution based on promissory estoppel. Because if he hadn't signed it you wouldn't have married him."

"That sounds very convoluted. And why are you reading up on contract law?"

"One of the newest members of my father's congregation is an attorney from Philadelphia."

"That still doesn't explain why you've been reading up on contract law."

Now Maude's cheeks were flushed too. "I wanted to have a topic of conversation when I speak to him."

"What are you speaking to him about?"

Maude shrugged and rubbed a blade of glass between her fingers. "I don't know. Father invited him to dinner after church next week and requested my attendance."

"So you wouldn't be opposed to marriage, just not marriage finagled by one of the women back there." Perry pointed vaguely over her shoulder.

"I think I'd still be opposed," Maude said reflectively. "But he's very handsome. And he has kind eyes."

"You're smitten."

Maude vehemently shook her head. "No. Not yet. But I could be. I'll let you know after Sunday dinner."

"Am I smitten too? Is that why I want to go back there and ogle Dio's backside?"

Maude smiled gently. "I think you've always been smitten with him. When we were younger, every conversation referred back to him in some way. I also think that's the reason you were so venomous toward him."

"I'll admit I've always found him handsome. That blue-black hair and those eyes. Brown with flecks of topaz and jade."

"And now you find him more than handsome."

It wasn't a question because she had been talking about ogling his rump. "Nigh irresistible. I need to keep my distance."

"Or maybe you just need to see what happens."

"I don't know if I even have that luxury. Mother warned me away. Rather ferociously."

Maude snorted derisively. "All the more reason to pursue whatever it is. Your mother is odious."

"Fine, let's go see if the ice cream is finished," Perry said as she offered her hand to her friend.

Dio was walking in their direction when they emerged from the grove of trees. His sleeves were still rolled to the elbows, and he wore a straw boater. He lifted a hand to shield his eyes when he saw her.

His gaze raked over her and made Perry intensely aware of the way her sweat had pooled between her shoulder blades. "I saved the two of you some ice cream," he said as soon as they were in hearing range.

"How in the world did you manage that?" Maude asked.

"I packed some in a metal pail and set it in the stream. Come on, I have spoons in my pocket."

"Is that a sanitary place to keep them?" Perry needled.

He swept her a sideways smile and winked. "I promise my shirt's clean, your majesty."

They followed him to the grove of trees on the other side of the field. The sound of the rushing water became louder as they drew closer, and the temperature on the bank was at least ten degrees cooler.

Perry wanted to dip her toes in it and flopped onto the bank to remove her shoes and stockings.

Just as Maude was dropping to the ground to copy her friend, a deep voice interrupted them. "Miss Latimer? Are you here? I thought I saw you walking in this direction."

Maude turned to Perry with wide eyes. "It's him. What should I do? And do I have anything stuck between my teeth?" Her friend asked as she stretched her mouth wide.

"You should answer him instead of sitting there like a ninny. And you don't have anything stuck between your teeth. This way you don't have to wait until Sunday to talk to him about contracts."

When Maude turned a panicked gaze to Dio, he nodded, affirming what Perry had said.

Maude scrambled up and brushed off her skirt. She raised a hand in farewell as she called out to the man calling for her. "I'm here, Mister Dempsey. I was just catching a breath of fresh air by the brook."

"Contracts?" Asked Dio, as soon as Maude had disappeared around the bend in the trail.

"She wanted to have a suitable topic of conversation at the ready."

Dio and Perry both burst into laughter. "Contracts are one of the most boring topics of conversation ever," Dio observed when he was finally able to catch his breath.

Perry shook her head in consternation. "I've never seen her so flustered."

"I think whoever this Mister Dempsey is, he's caught the attention of your best friend."

"It seems that way," Perry agreed. "I'm not complaining, because that means there's more ice cream for me."

"There were only two spoons - I thought we could give one to Maude and share the other one."

"Sharing a spoon is even more unsanitary than carrying one around in your pocket."

"Not any more unsanitary than kissing. And I might take liberties now our chaperone has abandoned us."

Chapter Eleven

Dio couldn't believe she'd stayed after Maude left. Especially after the comment he'd just made. But she gave him an unusually shy smile and continued to unroll her stockings. Once her feet were bare, she wriggled them against the grass and stretched her arms over her head. Dio couldn't look away.

"Would you like our ice cream now?" He cleared his throat and asked.

Her eyelids fluttered open and her gaze was the same iridescent jeweled green of the canopy of trees over their heads. "Ice cream sounds delightful," she said.

He pulled the pail from the water with the rope and smiled in satisfaction when he noted it was still cold to the touch.

"I didn't want to chance discovery with bowls, so we'll have to eat it straight from the pail."

She gave him a wistful smile. "That sounds like something we would have done as children. Life was so much simpler then."

He pried off the lid and held out her spoon. She cautiously approached him, but just as her fingers reached for her spoon, she tripped over a tree-root buried under the mound of crackling leaves. She sent them both sprawling, and Dio barely managed to hang onto the spoon he held.

Her fall had knocked hers from his hand and they watched as it arced into the air and landed in the middle of the stream with a splash.

Dio burst into laughter. "It appears we are sharing a spoon, Miss Trenton."

"Are you certain you didn't somehow engineer such a travesty?" She asked as she smiled down at him.

The sunlight filtering through the leaves cast a halo over her dark auburn hair, and her eyes sparkled with mischief. She was so achingly beautiful Dio felt his heart palpitate.

Her skirts were rucked halfway up her thighs, and the cotton of her pantaloons rubbed against his groin where she straddled him.

Dio masterfully tried to remain unaffected. His efforts were futile, and he hardened beneath her. She kept her eyes on his and moved her hips, ever so slightly.

He grew even harder, and he wondered if the rocking motion had made her wet. She leaned forward and he couldn't do anything but watch, mesmerized.

His spectacles, though askew, had miraculously remained attached. When she leaned forward to remove them he wanted to protest. When she carefully folded them, removed her hat and set them neatly inside it, his muscles quivered in anticipation of her next move.

He licked his lips. "The ice cream will melt," he weakly protested.

"The ice cream can withstand a five minute recess before it's devoured. But I don't think I can entertain such a delay, Dio Castellano."

"A delay?" He croaked.

"I tossed and turned all night for want of your kiss," she confessed as her mouth landed on the bridge of his nose before dusting over his cheekbones.

"I thought you'd decided against me."

"I did no such thing. Just because I am opposed to marriage does not mean I am opposed to the idea of doing *this* with you."

"What sort of this did you have in mind, Half-Pint?"

She grimaced at the nickname, just as he'd known she would. "There won't be any *this* if you don't call me by a new nickname."

"Besom?"

She thumped him in the chest.

"Termagant?"

She narrowed her eyes and pinched the skin at his wrist.

"Bane of my existence?"

"I might tolerate Bane. It has a certain conquering ring to it."

"Then Bane it is." He slid his hands under her body so he was cupping her. "Now kiss me, Bane, instead of merely threatening to do it."

She obediently dropped her lips to his. But no kiss ensued. She demonstrated exactly why she was the bane of his existence by trapping his bottom lip between her sharp little teeth. After she'd nipped him, she soothed away the hurt with her tongue. "There, I've blooded you for your insolence, knave," she murmured before she teased his mouth open with her own.

The sting she'd left on his lip was a haunting reminder of just how elusive she was. If she'd truly blooded him with her miniature act of savagery, he wanted to paint the scarlet across her breastbone, and wrap it around her wrists. Claim her with the salt copper scent of his veins.

When she shifted her hips, he tightened his hold. "If you don't hold still, you'll push me beyond the bounds of my endurance, Bane," he growled.

"Perhaps that is what I strive for, Dio. Especially if I receive a growl as my reward," she saucily retorted.

"Incorrigible," he grunted and in retaliation he pulled her further up his body, so the length of his cock pressed directly against her center. This time, when she moved, it was because Dio yanked her hips forward. They both groaned at the exquisite sensation.

He moved one of his hands and slid it into the opening of her pantaloons. She gasped into his mouth when the pad of his thumb stroked her clitoris, and bit his lip again. This time he knew it was an involuntary reaction to his caress instead of an expression of her bloodthirsty nature.

"I should deny you the release you're craving, since you refused my suit."

"You won't, because you want it as well," she murmured as she scraped her teeth along his jugular.

"Why would I want it? When you rejected my suit? When you're acting like a little succubus?"

"You've wanted it since that baseball game six years ago."

Dio tensed beneath her. "That was a long time ago. And nothing happened."

"If my brothers hadn't interrupted us, you would have kissed me. I saw it in your eyes."

"You saw no such thing," he protested.

"I may be innocent, Dio, but I'm not a fool. I felt the tug of war between us that day as well. I wanted you to kiss me - and I was disappointed when you didn't."

"I'll reward you for your confession. I want you to sit up and let me do most of the work."

She raised her body until she was perpendicular. "Now what? Where do I put my hands?"

"You can put your hands wherever you want."

When she slipped them inside his shirt and ran her fingernails across his chest, he flinched. She did it again and he rolled his body toward hers, so he was grinding against her for a full five seconds before he lowered his hips.

She abandoned her torture and arched her back. "Again," she demanded.

He braced himself on his elbows and held the position even longer this time. She grabbed a fistful of his shirt and rocked over him, keening.

"Hush," he admonished. "There's an entire field of people on the other side of those trees."

She bit her lip and he instantly wanted to soothe it. Her eyes were like glittering shards, translucent with the tears of her impending release.

When she began moaning he held his wrist to her mouth. She sank her teeth into it as she bucked astride him. She surged forward and let go of his shirt, tangling her fingers in his hair. Dio could feel the pulse of her release against his trousers as he closed his eyes and lost the last shred of his control.

Now he had no choice about returning to the party until the evidence of his undoing was dry. Unless he made it look like he'd had an impromptu swim in all his clothes.

All Dio wanted at the moment was a nap in the warm sunlight with this woman sprawled over his chest.

She dropped her head to his shoulder. "I never want to move," she confessed.

"I promised you chocolate ice cream. And I went to great lengths to get it. I made it with my own sweat and muscle, and I had to fend off both the quilting circle and Archie."

"What excuse did you make?"

He ran his fingers through her loosened hair. "None. I simply dished up half and absconded with the rest."

"Devious," she giggled into the curve of his neck. "A prosecutor stealing from the community he should be serving."

"It was for a worthy cause. I think they'd forgive me if they knew the reason I was compelled to steal it."

She scratched circles around his navel through the fabric. "And what reason is that?"

"A reason as old as time. I needed it for wooing."

"You're very determined. Especially after I informed you I'm not susceptible to wooing."

"Let's have our ice cream and then take a dip in the stream. That would excuse our wrinkled clothing and adequately disguise any other evidence of our activities."

She wrinkled her nose and he wanted to kiss the adorable arch it made of her freckles. "The water will be cold."

"You won't catch a cold - it's too warm outside. Weren't you going to wade in before I distracted you with a promise of ice cream?"

"It's much easier to warm my toes than it is to warm my entire body."

"I have flint in the picnic basket over there," Dio pointed to the basket they'd nearly crushed when they toppled to the ground. "I'll dig a fire pit to warm you if I need to."

She stood and fluttered her lashes at him again. "That's much more romantic than bringing me a bouquet of flowers."

"I should have listened to Archie," Dio grumbled. "He told me you didn't like flowers but I convinced myself he was wrong."

"He was wrong," she said as she threw her arms around his neck and delivered a peck to his cheek. "I love bouquets just like the one you gave me. Daisies and roses, so the inclusion of too many scents didn't overwhelm me and cause a sneezing fit."

"Count on you to have a no-nonsense approach to courting."

"If this is your idea of courting, Diogenes Castellano," she purred in his ear. "I approve."

They ended up feeding each other ice cream. And then licking it from each other's bodies. Perry had quivered and made an unholy sound when he'd placed dollops across the tops of her breasts and suckled them once the melting path was dripping from her nipples. The cold had made them hard as marbles against his tongue and he'd made her thrash when he made sure she was licked clean.

The stream had been even more welcome after that interlude. They'd both stepped into it fully clothed, and ducked under the rippling water to wash away the scent of how their afternoon was spent.

The picnic was in an uproar when they returned. Agatha Trenton was facing off the town's first lady, who had her unmarried daughter pinned to her side. Though her jaw was tight, Perry's mother was coolly unruffled. By contrast, the other woman's face and neck were more vibrantly red than a ripe tomato and she looked as if an apoplexy was imminent.

As soon as Dio and Perry strolled into view the woman thrust a finger in her direction. "There she is in the flesh! The moral corruption in our midst! The unabashed harlot!"

"My daughter is none of those things. I'm sure your daughter is lying about the origins of her little pamphlet."

Dio's hand tightened around hers. Perry had been afraid this reckoning would come, she'd just thought she'd have more time to figure out how to beat it.

She loosened her hand from that of her escort and stepped forward. "I'd like to know what I'm being accused of."

Mrs. Smith, the mayor's wife, turned to her and began screeching. "You degenerate! You've polluted my daughter's mind with the filth you're purveying. I'll see you investigated."

"The Willow Creek Crier is not filth."

"I'm not talking about the newspaper, girl, and well you know it." The woman's eyes were beady, like those of a cornered rodent, as she shook her finger in Perry's direction. "I'm talking about the slop you've tried to disguise with recipes. The slop you're distributing as part of your alleged Women's Improvement Society. I saw the diagrams."

She heard the swift intake of breath behind her and knew this was exactly the confrontation Dio had warned her about. "The diagrams and the other information in the pamphlet are meant to enlighten and educate the women of Willow Creek."

"I've called the constable. He should be here shortly to place you under arrest," Mrs. Smith triumphantly informed her.

The woman's gaze drifted behind her. "It appears you were in the intimate, unchaperoned company of the town prosecutor. I wonder if we can trust him to mete out justice."

Her insinuation was snide, and Perry could practically feel the waves of fury rolling off Dio. "Mrs. Smith, you have no cause to doubt I will uphold the integrity of my office," he said in a clipped, dangerous tone.

"If that's the case, why are you both soaked to the bone? As if you've been cavorting in the river?"

To Perry's relief, she was spared a reply. "I'm certain my daughter has a reasonable explanation for the state of her clothing."

"I lost my footing when I waded into the stream. Mr. Castellano came upon me floundering about and thought I needed assistance. He lost his footing as well," Perry brazenly lied.

Dio didn't correct her version of events and she wondered if he'd somehow just perjured himself.

"What seems to be the problem?" The constable sounded annoyed.

"Eloise," the mayor's wife turned to her daughter. "Show the constable why I've summoned him."

The girl, who at nineteen was considered an adult, pulled one of the pamphlets from where she'd had it sandwiched in her bodice. She thrust it in the direction of the constable.

He perused it for a moment, before he glared over at the mayor's wife. "Since when are recipes for pie crust a reason to demand my intervention?"

"Open the document to its final page," Mrs. Smith crisply instructed.

When he did, his whole face turned red. "This is not for public consumption," he muttered.

"You'll arrest Miss Trenton for violating the Comstock Act. It prohibits the distribution of obscene material."

The constable turned to Perry. "Miss Trenton, are you responsible for this chicanery?"

Perry feared what would happen to Maude if she was implicated as well, so there was no hope for it. "I am," she said past the lump of fear in her throat.

The man's expression tightened. "By the authority vested in me as an officer of the law, I'm placing you under arrest for the violation of public standards of decency. You may come with me of your own accord, or I can restrain you and bring you before the magistrate by force."

"I'll come willingly."

"If you so desire, you may seek counsel from an attorney of your choosing."

"I'll be giving her counsel." Dio's statement brooked no argument.

"Mr. Castellano, you too, are an officer of the court. You cannot offer counsel to the accused unless you are appointed to do so. Which you will not be because you will be on the opposing side of the bench."

"Then I resign my post."

"Dio, no. I won't let you," Perry hissed. "I understand the conditions of my arrest and the charges levied against me, Constable."

"Perry, let me help you," Dio pleaded behind her.

"Now isn't the time, Mr. Castellano," she said over her shoulder as she followed the constable to his waiting wagon.

Chapter Twelve

THE MAGISTRATE WAS SUMMONED almost immediately after Perry was placed in one of the cells. When she was summoned for her arraignment, the constable handcuffed her. "It's not that I believe you're a violent criminal, Miss Trenton, it's protocol."

As Perry stood in front of the man who'd frequently dined at their table, she rubbed her wrists where they chafed against the iron.

The magistrate peered at her over the glasses perched on the end of his nose. "Miss Trenton, are you aware of the gravity of your situation?"

"I understand that I have been accused of violating the municipal laws enacted to mirror the Comstock Act."

"Yes. A serious offense, madam, and one I would not have expected from someone of your station. The punishment for your violation could result in a prison sentence of up to ten years." He ran his hand over his face and removed his glasses. "May I ask what possessed you to act so recklessly?"

"I was not acting recklessly, sir. The material I distributed was educational in nature. It's meant to give women a better understanding of their bodies."

"The material not only contained graphic illustrations, Miss Trenton, it included graphic language that described certain acts in detail. Acts that should not be discussed outside the sanctity of the marriage bed."

"May I ask a question, sir?"

He waved a hand for her to proceed.

"Are men not given access to this information?"

The magistrate sighed. "It is not the same, Miss Trenton, and well you know it. As men, we are more bound to our animal nature and its urges. It is up to women to tame those urges, not inflame them."

"So you believe pleasure has no place in procreation?" Perry badgered.

The magistrate's face flushed in embarrassment. "Miss Trenton, I believe a publicly distributed pamphlet is not the appropriate means to discuss such issues. I'm allowing you a trial by your peers, but I would suggest you find competent legal counsel."

As the magistrate was tapping the lectern with his gavel, the door burst open.

Dio's clothes were dry, but he looked windblown and furious.

"Ah, Mr. Castellano. You'll need to prepare a case against Miss Trenton."

"I will not. Although she hasn't accepted my offer, I have asked her to marry me. My feelings are intimately engaged and I cannot remain objective. I am recusing myself that I may serve as her legal counsel instead."

"This is highly unusual. You said you've asked this woman to marry you, so you know her well. Correct, Mr. Castellano?"

"Yes, our families have been friends my entire life."

"Then you are in a unique position. Rather than sending Miss Trenton back to a cell to await trial, I am releasing her into your custody."

"My custody? Isn't it highly irregular to release an unmarried woman to the household of a bachelor?"

"Given the nature of Miss Trenton's offense, and what she's been accused of, I believe her reputation is already damaged beyond repair. Once the constable releases her from her restraints, you may convey her to your home."

His impatience was tangible, and as soon as the constable released her, he strode forward and cradled her wrists. "I'll tend to these when you're safe," he vowed as his eyes searched hers. "Are you hurt in any other way?"

Perry shook her head and blinked away the sudden sheen of tears. His eyes were glassy as well, shimmering and intense behind his spectacles. "Just exhausted from the ordeal, and feeling bedraggled."

"Come," he said and put his arm around her shoulders.

Perry leaned her head into the hard frame of his shoulder, grateful for his support. She realized in that moment that he was the one person she wanted there. He was nothing but solicitous and gentle, and she knew her mother's reaction, and likely that of her father would have been just the opposite. Censorious and demeaning. Making her feel ashamed of her actions and adding to the humiliation of the experience.

Perry knew from Dio's actions that his opinion of her remained unchanged. Although he saw her as reckless, he also saw her as strong and resilient. As a woman in charge of all her faculties and designed to weather the storm that approached them.

He'd brought his closed carriage and she was shocked to see her brother in the driver's seat. Archie's smile gleamed down at her. It was uncharacteristically soft and bore none of his usual wry humor. "Dio and I will get you out of this mess, Half-Pint."

Perry was so overwhelmed by his show of loyalty, she didn't protest his use of the childhood nickname she loathed.

Dio's hands lingered at her waist as he propelled her into the carriage, and after he'd closed the door, he tugged her onto his lap.

She struggled for a moment - until he kissed the crown of her head. "Don't deny me this, Bane. I need to hold you right now. To know you're safe."

Perry acquiesced, laying her head on his shoulder. "I'm afraid," she admitted. "But I'm not ashamed."

"You shouldn't be ashamed. The men who wrote those laws should be ashamed. There is nothing in our natural inclination to explore our bodies that we should be forced to ignore or hide. What you are providing is educational - but it's also empowering. You're arming women with the resources they should have always had."

"Not everyone thinks as you do. It's glaringly obvious there is a substantial population of Anti-Suffragists here in Willow Creek, my mother chief among their number."

"Even Anti-Suffragists should be grateful for the knowledge you are providing - because it leads directly to domestic bliss. I'll bet there are plenty of them that subscribe to your pamphlet and attend your meetings."

"But how do I make them see that what I'm doing is helping them rather than harming them? How do I persuade them to have frank conversations with their husbands, who will be appointed to a jury that assesses my guilt?"

He must have sensed her feeling of helplessness, because he smoothed his hand down her spine and pressed a lingering kiss to her temple. "Let me handle speaking to the men who'll be called to pass judgment on your actions."

"I feel so overwhelmed," she confessed in a small voice, as the turmoil of the day's events finally made itself felt.

"Three weeks ago, in that alley, I said I wanted to protect you. I meant it, Perry. Even if you don't want my protection or think it's unnecessary or gratuitous."

"I don't like to depend on anyone other than myself. It makes me feel weak."

His laughter rumbled beneath her ear. "Bane, you are the strongest woman I know. Nothing about you is weak," he said as he massaged the base of her spine. "But even the strongest of us cannot do everything by themselves. You can lean on me without fearing I'll violate your trust."

Perry didn't know what to do with his declaration, so she let it sink into her bones. Into her heart. As his scent of cedar and fresh water and spring washed over her, she privately acknowledged she'd been fighting against the way he made her feel, determined to deny it and relegate it to the back of her mind. That afternoon, she'd recognized the futility of her efforts. He was hooked in her soul like a harpoon. He'd always been there.

The only other time Perry had been to Dio's home was under cover of darkness, so she hadn't appreciated its grandeur. As he lifted her from the carriage she squared her shoulders.

Her parents stood on the top step, their expressions unreadable.

When her mother saw her, she flinched.

"We've come to discuss your part in this fiasco, young man," Perry's father addressed Dio.

"What is the meaning of this? Why is my daughter in your company?" Her mother demanded.

Neither of her parents glanced in her direction, and spoke of her as if she wasn't standing before them. It was just another way they made her feel diminutive.

"Whatever you're going to say to Mr. Castellano you may say to me as well," she told them.

"Then explain to me why you've endangered your livelihood, and sullied the reputation of our name, with your illicit activities."

Perry had rarely seen her father so angry. His hand was white-knuckled where it gripped his walking stick, and his expression was grim.

Dio's hand in the small of her back reminded her she had the strength and courage to defy her father and his edicts. "If the cost of aiding my gender in the pursuit of equal treatment and self-reliance is my business, then I gladly sacrifice it. I have done nothing to warrant your disapproval, only sought to employ the empathy and pragmatism you instilled in me."

"As your father will corroborate, Pericles, empathy has no place in commerce," her mother pointed out with an implacable look.

Her father cleared his throat, and she saw something like both pride and resignation pass over his face. "No, Agatha, I won't corroborate your assumption. Our daughter is right. She is only putting into practice the lessons I've taught her."

Her mother sputtered at his side, "But, Arthur! Her antics jeopardize our social standing!"

He turned to his wife and firmly shook his head. "No. Our children and their well-being will always be more important than your social calendar and connections. We will do everything in our power as one unit to see our daughter on the other side of this."

He grasped her arm and urged her down the steps, still sputtering. After he'd lifted her into the carriage Perry now realized was theirs, her father speared Dio with a resolute gaze. "I am placing my daughter's fate in your hands, young man. Do not disappoint me."

Archie tipped his hat to them and gave his best friend a pointed look. "I trust you not to take advantage of her," he warned before he slapped the reins against the rump of the horse and crooned, "Giddyap."

Perry watched the carriage disappear around the bend in the road in disbelief. "My father has never stood up for me, or seemed proud of me."

Dio slid his arm around her waist. "He's clearly proud of you, Bane. Perhaps it was harder for him to acknowledge since your accomplishments aren't typical of daughters, or what he expected of you."

"Are you going to take advantage of me?" Perry asked him in a muffled tone.

"I think I've already taken enough advantage for one day. I'm going to pour you a bath and bring you some bourbon."

Perry sighed. "That sounds lovely." It felt like the grime that had coated the floors and walls of the cell had seeped into her skin. She wanted to scrub it off. And the bourbon would settle the knot of anxiety and dread in her stomach - mellow it so she could muster her defenses.

He escorted her up the winding staircase to the second floor.

Perry breathed a sigh of appreciation when she saw the bathing room. The floor and ceiling were tiled in pastel mosaics and the walls were outfitted with mirrors. The white porcelain clawfoot tub was wide enough and deep enough for more than one person to comfortably stretch out.

"I'd indulge in a luxurious bath every morning," she confessed.

"The taps have a steady supply of hot water from the boiler in the basement, so you may indulge to your heart's content while you're here."

Perry lifted her foot to the stool at the edge of the tub so she could unlace her boot. When she looked over her shoulder to ask him if he had any rosemary for her hair, his eyes were molten and glued to her posterior. "Would you like to undress me?" She asked coquettishly.

"Hells, yes. I'd like nothing more," he said as he prowled toward her.

She abandoned her half-tied laces at his approach, her whole body suddenly sparking from his heated gaze.

He crouched in front of her and lifted her booted foot to his thigh. When he slid his fingers around her ankle inside the leather, and then ran his knuckles over the bare skin of her calf, gooseflesh trailed over her skin in the wake of his touch. He swiftly unlaced her boot and set his thumb against the arch of her foot. Her muscles were tender there, and the massage loosened something inside her. He set her foot on his other knee and reached for her other boot.

He repeated the process, and by the time he moved to the row of buttons down the front of her calico, she was half-asleep.

Once he'd peeled the outer layer of clothes from her body, his hands cupped her shoulders, massaging the sore muscles there as he'd ministered to her feet. She tipped her head back and moaned in relief. "You're nothing but clay in my arms right now, Bane. Not the little wildcat with claws and teeth I'm used to," he said as he grazed the tip of her ear with his mouth.

Perry's head felt muzzy, her bones lighter than air. "I promise I won't fall asleep in the tub," she mumbled.

He unlaced the ribbons that secured her chemise and turned her around so he could pull it and the attached pantalets from her body. She let him, her body pliant as that of one of the rag dolls she'd played with as a girl. "I don't want to risk you drowning, so I'll sit on the stool and scrub your back."

Perry's eyes flickered open briefly. "My arms feel like lead weights - will you wash my hair as well?"

"I've dreamt of your wet hair plastered against me, so yes, Bane, I'll wash your hair."

"I need to decide on a nickname for you," Perry murmured.

"I'm going to ensure you have the rest of our lives to devise one," he proclaimed.

His words registered, but Perry wasn't in the mood to disabuse him of such a fanciful declaration.

When he lifted her into his arms and sat on the stool to turn on the spigots, she drifted off again. Moments, or hours later, the warm water enveloped her, soothing the ache in her limbs.

"Tip your head forward," he instructed from behind her.

She obeyed, and rested the side of her face against her raised knees as he poured a glass of water over her head. "I have a honey and vinegar mix to cleanse your hair."

"That's what I use at home."

"It's what my sisters use as well. Aspasia left it here when she was decorating the parlor."

When his lean fingers gripped her scalp, the sensation was decadent. He held her nape in one palm and worked the mix through each strand, and tipped her forward again when he'd finished so he could rinse it away.

When he was satisfied, he pushed her forward again and lathered the sponge. He moved it over her back in long, broad strokes, until she felt like she was going to float away.

"What about the rest of my body?"

He feathered a kiss across her nape. "I don't trust myself to attend to the rest of you without seeking my own pleasure," he rasped.

"I wouldn't protest."

He inhaled. "As you wish, wildcat."

The sponge glided over her collarbones before dipping beneath the water to draw languid circles over her breasts. She moved restlessly beneath the water, her knees falling open of their own volition. "So fucking perfect," he praised as he dipped his tongue in her ear. He swirled it for a moment before nipping her earlobe.

He set the sponge on the side of the tub and filled his hands with her, letting his thumbs graze the tight furl of her nipples. Perry surged into that captive touch. "Let me ease the last of your tension," he groaned as he dipped one hand beneath the water and stroked it down the length of her torso. He swept a path across her navel, and then brushed two fingers over her swollen arousal. His touch was a lick of flame down the center of her body, and when he plunged his fingers inside her, she bowed her back and gripped the sides of the tub. He held her fast. "You're almost there, Bane. Let it go," he coaxed, his voice like raw silk.

Chapter Thirteen

SHE WAS LIKE A forbidden banquet laid out before him, and Dio shifted on the stool to ease his aching cock. This wasn't about him or his needs. For the second time that day he sacrificed them at her altar. He should have bundled her immediately into a bed and insisted she take a bath in the morning. He needed distance and a clear head so he could strategize about her defense.

But when he felt the pulse of her release as she clenched around his fingers, he went white-hot with want.

"Hold onto the sides of the tub," he instructed as he rose from the stool and moved to face her. He left the shirt on, too rushed to bother with it, but made short work of his trousers. Once he'd kicked them away, he took himself in hand. "Watch, little wildcat. Watch how you turn me inside out," Dio commanded as he gripped his cock. He tightened his fingers around the broad head, closing his eyes as he fisted his length. He imagined flipping her over and pushing her to her knees, caging her body from behind as he spread her open and plunged into her tight heat.

Her eyes were glazed as she watched him, and even though he'd felt her release, she dropped one of her hands beneath the water. The flex of her arm sent a lighting bolt through him, and he bit his lower lip as he covered her breasts and stomach with his release.

He used the voluminous length of his shirt to wipe himself clean and then leaned forward to dip it into the water between her legs. When the wet cotton that covered his knuckles slid over her center she shivered. "How can I want your touch again so soon?" She plaintively asked.

"Because you know I'll meet your needs, Bane," he answered as he wiped his seed from her skin. "I'll not apologize for your need to rewash."

She arched a brow and grabbed the sponge. "I wouldn't ask you to."

Her brazen answer made him want to join her in the tub. To do the kinds of things to her he'd imagined doing. But he wasn't going to be selfish. He pressed a reverent kiss to her forehead and stepped away.

"I'm going to put fresh linens on the bed. I'll be back to retrieve you in a quarter of an hour."

He hurried through his chores. He set the teapot on the stove and smoothed the sheets he grabbed from the closet onto his bed. She wouldn't be occupying a guest room.

He needed the sweetness of her curled in his arms while he slept.

When Dio was finished, he crept into the bathing chamber, hoping to catch her in an unguarded moment. Her head was tipped back against the rim of the tub, her cheeks flushed. While he was gone, she'd somehow managed to plait her hair into a long braid that dangled over one breast. The water had cooled, but the steam had left its mark in the curls plastered against her forehead and cheeks.

She didn't stir until he knelt and swept her dripping body into his arms. When he set her atop his feet so he could swing her in the direction of the towel he'd left in front of the fire, she laughed and twined her arms around his neck.

She was blissfully drowsy, glowing and gorgeous, and he wanted to make her irrevocably his. Archie's parting admonition echoed in his head as he rubbed her vigorously with the warmed linen. He wouldn't take advantage of her more than he had. If she wanted more from their relationship, he'd leave the decision to her.

He scooped her into his arms. "Come along, sleeping beauty. Your enchanted berth awaits."

Within moments of tucking her in, her gentle snores filled the room. He'd have to remember to tease her about it later.

When he turned up the glass lamp and reached for his text on criminal procedure and allowable defenses, he missed her. The cozy study that had seemed like a haven now just seemed empty. He wanted to ascend the stairs and pull her flush against him, to fall asleep with the scent of her honeyed hair in his nostrils. But he had a case to prepare. The most important one of his life.

The pounding on the door woke him up. He'd fallen asleep with his head in a book. His back was stiff and his muscles cramped, and when he yawned he tasted the bourbon in the back of his throat. He plucked his spectacles from the shelf behind him and slid them over his nose.

When Dio flung open the door, Archie stood there.

"Is my sister still asleep?" he asked as he brushed past.

"I think so. She's in my bed."

Archie raised a brow and Dio hurried to lay to rest his protective instincts. "I slept in my study." *Dio was not going to tell his best friend what had transpired before he laid her to rest.*

"Keep your secrets, friend," Archie said as he thumped Dio's shoulder. "I want to hear what you think about the charges levied against Pericles."

Dio grinned. "I think we can easily defeat them. The premise of the Comstock Act, and all the parochial legislation based on it, is that each community determines its own decency standards."

Archie's brow furrowed. "How is that a good thing when you have women like Mrs. Smith in the community?"

"It's helpful because although her voice may be one of the loudest, it isn't necessarily the voice of the majority. Have you read your sister's pamphlets?"

"No," his friend said as he wrinkled his nose. "I'm afraid to."

"Well, you should. Your sister is brilliant. She used a series of diary entries she translated from the original Italian, with some strange references in places, to demonstrate to women how to enhance their pleasure in the marriage bed. Her pamphlets aren't encouraging salacious behavior or fornication. They're giving wives a way to keep their husbands from straying."

"But women can't serve on a jury."

"No - but their satisfied husbands can. I need to look at the distribution logs your sister kept, but she told me she had hundreds of subscribers."

Archie's eyes lit up. "And there are less than a thousand households in Willow Creek."

"Exactly," Dio said as he rubbed his hands together. "Which means the majority of the men who will be called to serve on the jury have likely reaped the benefits of those pamphlets."

"Which also means they wouldn't categorize them as obscene."

Dio nodded. "Unless they're hypocrites. If they are, I can ferret it out during voir dire."

After Dio had ushered Archie up the stairs and could hear the muted rumble of the siblings' conversation, he extracted a sheaf of paper and began to write.

When he finished hours later, the afternoon sun was already low on the horizon and his hand was cramped.

"I've been watching you for the last half hour," a siren's voice said. "You were oblivious to my presence," his houseguest finished as she sank into the settee across from his desk.

"Last night I figured out how to mount our defense."

She pulled her knees to her chin, so the folds of the robe she'd pulled on pooled around her body. The bright turquoise color was reflected in her eyes, and she kicked off his slippers as she tucked her bare feet beneath the draped material. He'd never accustom himself to the way her mere presence, and most innocuous gestures, rendered him immobile.

"Are you tongue-tied? You may continue."

Dio closed his eyes and gripped the edge of the desk behind him to steady his whirling thoughts. "Remember when I said I'd talk to the men who'll be recruited for jury duty?"

"Yes. I assume you have a strategy for approaching them?"

"The charges against you are for violating the portion of Willow Creek's municipal code that lays out community decency standards. Those standards are vague, and when someone's accused of violating them, the burden to prove the act or material is obscene is in the hands of the prosecution. The only way something can be determined obscene is if the community itself decides it constitutes an affront to its standards of decency."

Perry nodded in understanding. "So the jury will determine if the pamphlets are obscene. And most, if not all, of the men appointed to the jury have wives who are subscribers and have probably employed the instructions the pamphlets provided to the benefit of their husbands."

"Yes. So our defense is straightforward. You marketed the pamphlets as marriage aids, and that's how we'll present them. Any unmarried individuals that read the pamphlets likely obtained them through distribution channels outside your purview."

"It's brilliant. You're brilliant," she said as she rose to her feet.

Dio was acutely aware she wore nothing beneath his robe. He grasped the end of the loosely tied belt and tugged her close. "You appreciate me."

"I appreciate you and I admire you. I'm still averse to the shackles of marriage, but I wouldn't be averse to enjoying some of the benefits that venerable institution provides."

"Such as?" He asked as he reeled her firmly into his arms.

"Such as this," she elaborated as she wrapped her hand over him.

He could feel the individual press of each finger through his trousers, and surged against her.

"Will you show me those benefits, Dio?"

He closed his eyes again and clenched his jaw. "I made a vow to myself. That I wouldn't be selfish."

She unbuttoned him with one hand and used the other one to pull his face down to hers. "What if I'm the one who's being selfish?" She taunted as her fingers glided across his lower stomach.

"Why do you insist on goading me? I'm trying to be a paragon of virtue."

"Dio," she laughingly chastised. "That carriage ran away a long time ago. I know you have no desire to be virtuous, at least not where I'm concerned. I want to see what you're like under that polite mask of indifference you show everyone else. I want you to let go - to show me you're passionate about something besides closing arguments."

"I'm passionate, Perry. But passion is dangerous. It undermines rational thought and can imbalance the scales of justice."

"Tell me why you wanted the judge to release me into your custody."

Dio's epiphany, that he was irrevocably in love with her, wasn't something he was ready to share. He whirled them around, and flattened his palms on the desk, caging her in. "I didn't trust anyone else to take care of you."

"You haven't taken care of anything," she insisted as she cupped his jaw. Silently conveying exactly what she needed him to take care of.

"Not for lack of trying," he muttered before she found his lips on hers.

"I dreamt of kissing you again, while I was up there lying in your bed. I wanted to feel the brush of your mustache against my upper lip and the scratch of your jaw beneath my hands."

"Will you let me take care of you, Perry?" He asked softly as the warmth of his breath rippled over her skin.

Chapter Fourteen

Perry nodded her assent and tipped her head back further. He cupped her nape in his palm and massaged the taut muscles at the base of her neck. "This is why I wanted you in my custody, Perry. So you could tell me what you want. So you could show me how to please you."

His nimble touch brushed aside the robe and trailed up her ribcage. Once he'd spread the garment wide, so it framed the rise of her breasts and the slight undulation of her stomach he groaned in appreciation.

"God, I've dreamt of your breasts. Spent hours with my cock in my hand imagining their color and taste and texture. Finish undressing me, Perry." He demanded with a hooded gaze.

Her hand trembled as she reached for his waistband.

She flicked the row of buttons open and yanked the pants over the curve of his ass.

"You've dreamt of my breasts and I've dreamt of biting this," She said as she grabbed a handful of flesh. "It's solid muscle, and whenever you swing onto your horse, or crouch or bend, it's a battle to hold myself back."

He pressed her hard against the edge of the desk. "Are you already wet for me?"

He grasped her wrist and moved her hand to her front. He trailed their twined fingers down her torso, his gold-flecked brown eyes pure sin beneath the gaslight, pinning her in place. His thumb pressed hers against her core, forcing them both to rub small circles all around her clitoris.

Perry melted beneath the languor of their joint touch, her body undulating against the wooden surface behind her. "Lie back, Bane, and let me taste you."

As Perry reclined against the unforgiving surface she wondered if he'd read the entire pamphlet.

"*Bagna le mie dita, gatta selvatica*," he said as he dropped to his knees.

He'd just called her wildcat and told her to soak his fingers. In Italian. She should have asked for his help translating the diaries.

"*Succosa*," he murmured against her thigh. "*Liscia*," he continued as his tongue swept over her vulva.

Juicy. Slick.

She knew Italian was his first language, but she'd never heard him speak it. She'd never imagined him speaking it like this. Worshipfully. Filthily.

"*Posso entrare, gatta selvatica?*" May I come in, wildcat? He growled against her center.

"*Sii mio ospite.*" Be my guest, she purred like her namesake and tangled her hands in his dark locks.

He slid his tongue inside her and her legs curled around his shoulders. She hooked her ankles behind his head and arched her back as he stroked a spot that made the room spin. His thumb returned to its resting place, pressing her hand against her greedy center. He maneuvered her wrist as his tongue wreaked havoc with the last shreds of her control. When he lifted his mouth and scraped his teeth over her arousal, she came apart.

"*Voglio di più, vuoi entrare?*" She asked as she leaned forward to cradle his jaw. I want more, will you come inside?

His eyes searched hers as he swiped the back of his hand across his mouth. "*Ti proteggero. Anche da me stesso.*" I'll protect you. Even against myself.

Perry tightened her grip on his jaw, her gaze fierce. "*Voglio questo. Voglio questo con te.*" I want this. I want this with you.

He closed his eyes and clenched his fists. "*Sono impotente contro di te.*" I am helpless against you.

He pulled open a drawer to the right of where she sat and removed a slim metal box. He lifted a condom from the inside of it and held it out. "*Me lo metti?*" Will you put it on me?

Perry took it from him and wrestled his trousers to his knees. "*Sì.*" Yes, I will.

She slowly slid the rubber over his cock, brushing her knuckles over every ridge and vein. "*Sarai la mia fine,*" he groaned.

You'll be the end of me.

He would be the end of her if he didn't do as she asked.

"*Subito,*" Perry pleaded. Now. She needed him now.

He tilted her head back, his broad palm fanning the side of her jaw and the back of her neck. He scraped his teeth along her pulse and surged forward.

There was a pinch of discomfort and then she was full of him. "*Preziosa. Mia amata.*" He groaned as he dropped his head to her shoulder.

Precious. Beloved.

The true reason she was in his custody. The true reason he was doing everything in his power to protect her. She wrapped her legs around his waist and kissed his palm. "*Solo per te,*" she whispered. Only for you.

He stilled inside her, his forearms taut, the muscles of his neck and shoulders rigid with holding back. "*Voglio che duri,*" I want it to last, he said as he kissed the corners of her mouth and the tip of her nose.

Perry made the decision for him, clenching her inner thighs and her inner muscles around his length. Her subtle movement was all the encouragement he needed. She felt the jerk of his cock as he filled the condom with his seed, and rubbed circles over his back, crooning as he rested his forehead against hers.

They didn't speak of what had happened, but he carried her upstairs and curled his arm around her waist in his bed. Like a toasty giant spoon.

When Perry woke, he wasn't there. She could still smell him in the sheets, and the indentation in the mattress where he'd been laying was still warm.

When she heard his footsteps on the stairs she tried to smooth the tangles from her hair. He sat on the edge of the bed and handed her a cup of steaming tea.

She wrapped both hands around it and sighed at taste. He'd made it with cream and sugar, just as she liked it. She knew he preferred coffee - which meant he'd made it especially for her.

"I don't think there will be a trial."

"How did you manage that?"

"I filed a motion to dismiss with the magistrate. On the grounds that your pamphlet doesn't meet the community standards for obscenity and the citation is without grounds."

"Do you think it will work?"

"Yes. But the court will probably require you to cease and desist from distributing any more of them."

"It's knowledge the women of Willow Creek both want and need."

"I have an idea. I'm still working out the details, but we can devise a plan once we meet with the magistrate."

"Is he expecting us soon?"

He nodded. "This afternoon. I gave him my motion this morning and he said he'd give me a decision by three o' clock. Your mother had a valise of clothing delivered."

Perry drained the last of the tea and set aside the mug. "Our styles are vastly different. I shudder to think what she packed."

"As long as we both look more respectable than we did yesterday, I'm sure it will be fine."

Perry's gaze roamed over him. He was wearing one of his ubiquitous black coats with matching trousers. But he'd foregone the tie. His shirt was open at the collar and she could see the strong, golden column of his throat.

She leaned forward before he could retreat and did what she'd wanted to do for months. She scraped her teeth over his Adam's apple.

He growled and tumbled her backward. "Gatta selvatica," he rumbled in her ear.

"Grande gallo," Perry replied.

Dio lifted his head. "Are you calling me a big rooster or complimenting my cock?" He laughingly asked. "That's not how you would pay me such an insult or a compliment."

Perry shrugged and giggled. "Maybe I was trying to call you both?"

He smoothed her hair from her forehead and pressed a kiss there. "Though I appreciate the sentiment, preziosa, it lacks your signature originality. I demand another nickname."

Chapter Fifteen

THE MAGISTRATE REGARDED THEM from across the daunting expanse of his walnut desk with steepled fingers. "I spoke to my wife last night."

Perry wondered where the conversation was going and held her breath.

"She subscribes to your pamphlets, Miss Trenton. She informed me they are the reason we have both been more invigorated of late." His cheeks were ruddy beneath his mutton chops.

"Yes, your wife receives one of my pamphlets every two weeks."

He nodded brusquely in acknowledgment. "After our conversation, I began examining the case law. The majority of the cases that were fully prosecuted dealt with the distribution of contraceptives and the administration of both houses of ill repute and establishments where women sought out pregnancy terminations. This case falls into none of those categories. Additionally, the pamphlet specifically states the information contained therein is to be used to enhance the household and the marital relationship."

Dio breathed a sigh of relief beside her.

"However," the magistrate continued. "That still does not address the fact your pamphlet fell into the wrong hands. To prevent that from happening in the future, I am including a caveat in my dismissal order that requires you to confine the pamphlet's contents to actual household tips and recipes."

Perry nodded, both grateful and overwhelmed.

"Thank you, sir," Dio extended his right hand as he stood. The magistrate shook it.

"I hope to see you in court again next week, Mr. Castellano."

"I'll return after my honeymoon."

The man guffawed. "So Miss Trenton was not a charity case."

Perry's nerves were jumbled as they descended the steps and crossed the street to the waiting carriage.

When they were seated, she twisted her hands in her lap. "Honeymoon?" She croaked, once Dio threw himself onto the bench across from her.

"Yes, Bane. Honeymoon. I'm irrevocably, unabashedly in love with you. I have been since I almost kissed you on home plate. And I think you love me too."

"I've told you why I'm opposed to marriage."

He reached over and took her hands in his own, straightening her fingers and raising them to his lips for a kiss.

"I don't take your opposition lightly, so here are the terms. One - I sign what amounts to a quit claim deed once we're wed, that transfers all your business property and interests back to you. Or if you prefer, I'll sign a pre-nuptial agreement relinquishing all my marital rights to the assets you now possess. Two- I help you establish a bi-monthly salon that takes the place of the pamphlet. We can use the large parlor. Three - I promise to treat you with the respect you deserve. I will always ensure my actions take your intellectual and bodily autonomy into account. That includes respecting your wishes about the production of offspring - whatever they may be. Four - I'll become as devoted a woman's suffragist as you are, and use whatever resources I have available to recruit other men to our cause."

Perry's eyes watered. She'd never enjoyed the luxury of such unequivocal support. "I do love you," she admitted. "I've loved you since the day you collapsed by the home plate. I realized it then, when you went toppling to the ground, and I regretted I'd never told you."

"Then you'll agree to be my wife?" He asked as he pulled a box from his pocket and flipped it open.

The ring was peridot and onyx, and the gemstones all resembled elongated cat's eyes. "I'll agree if you meet my conditions."

"I'm afraid to commit without hearing them first," he laughed.

"I only have two. One - you help me translate the rest of the diaries. Your Italian is much better than mine and you can demonstrate what you've learned. Two - you let me call you *guance dolci*."

"Sweet cheeks? Are you trying to tell me you love my dimple or referencing the part of my anatomy you admitted you were tempted to bite? We need to work on your Italian."

She threw him a devilish grin. "I give you leave to instruct me if you accept my terms."

"I do." He said as he hauled her into his lap and slid the ring on her finger.

Note to Readers

I. Italian immigration and Thomas Jefferson

Most of the Italian-Americans that emigrated to the United States did so in the wake of political upheaval and economic uncertainty beginning in the last quarter of the nineteenth century. There were natives of Italy in the U.S. before that, but they only numbered in the ten thousands. One of the most notable communities I found was the Italian farmers who leased land from Thomas Jefferson. They were involved almost strictly in agriculture, and founded one of the oldest vineyards in Virginia.

It is these farmers and craftsmen that Dio is descended from.

II. The Comstock Act

The Comstock Act has been a topic in the news a lot lately. Especially for the implications it has for the accessibility of contraception and abortion. The law was originally the fruit of a morality crusade, and you can read more about how it began, what it entailed, and why it fell out of favor here:

https://www.pbs.org/wgbh/americanexperience/features/pill-anthony-comstocks-chastity-laws/

III. Anti-Suffragist Movement

Many women were opposed to women's suffrage, or any participation or representation of women in the political sphere. These women were typically members of the upper class and their beliefs were influenced by their distance from many of the struggles women who weren't protected by wealth and status endured. You can read more about what compelled these women to oppose the fight for women's rights here:

https://www.crusadeforthevote.org/naows-opposition

IV. Danville Massacre

The Danville Massacre was one of the first racial riots to happen in the wake of Reconstruction. It was stoked by members of the Funders political party who were opposed to the additional opportunities African Americans were granted when the Readjusters came into power. You can read more about it here:

https://encyclopediavirginia.org/entries/danville-riot-1883/

V. Readjuster Party/Democratic Party

As I was researching this novel, I was stunned by all the similarities in rhetoric, platform and sentiment the Funder and Readjuster parties had to the current political climate. It's also an enlightening dive into the fluctuating nature of party creeds and identities in this country.

https://encyclopediavirginia.org/entries/readjuster-party-the/

VI. The History of Ice Cream

We have my great grandmother's hand crank ice cream maker in our barn, and I wanted to incorporate some of those childhood memories. If you're an ice cream fan like me, you'll find this article entertaining:

https://www.idfa.org/the-history-of-ice-cream

About the author

Andrea loves writing sassy, independent women and complex, layered heroes who guard their hearts. She loves diving into obscure research and telling stories that readers don't expect to find.

She loves hearing from readers! You can email her at authorandreajenelle@gmail.com

You can find her books in your library via Hoopla and Libby and on all digital book platforms.

Also by Andrea

<u>Willow Creek Series (in order, but can be read in any order as standalones)</u>
No Regrets
No Surrender
No Promises
No Shadows
No Doubts
No Excuses
No Angels (Christmas novella in Kindle Unlimited)
Twelve Days & Twelve Nights (Christmas novella in the Wreck My Halls anthology)
No Apologies (releasing June 2025)
The Princess and the Clown (included in the Tangled Hearts anthology)
No Ghosts (Halloween novella releasing in the One Dark Night anthology Sept. 2025)

No Christmas Spirit (Christmas Novella releasing October 2025)
No Dreams (releasing October 2026)
No Strings (releasing June 2027)

<u>The Wainwright Sisters (Victorian era historical romance)</u>
When Araminta Greaves Traded Her Dignity for Bliss
How Frances Wainwright Learned to Love
Cece Wainwright's Christmas Wish
When Jess Wainwright's Curiosity was Satisfied (releasing Feb. 2025)
Handfasted in Haste (a holiday novella releasing November 2025)
How Gert Wainwright Spent Her Holiday (releasing Feb. 2026)
When Lavinia Wainwright Went Missing (releasing Feb. 2027)
Emily Wainwright's Exemplary Education (releasing November 2027)

<u>Sons & Daughters of Lir (paranormal urban romantasy inspired by Celtic mythology)</u>
Way Down We Go
Wither on the Vine
The Berserker's Daughter (prequel novella releasing August 2025)
Untitled Book 3 (releasing 2026)
Untitled Book 4 (releasing 2027)

<u>Starrlight Farms (a small town romance series set in Kentucky's Bluegrass region)</u>

Grace Above All (included in the Kentuckiana Romance Writers Anthology releasing in Fall 2025)

<u>The Terrible Trentons (a Victorian era small town romance series set in America)</u>

Spine of Steel (the first book in the Suffragette Uprising series, April 2025)

Nothing Compares to You (included in the Ordered Home Holiday Anthology, releasing Nov. 2025)

<u>Standalones</u>

What the Season Brings (a 1990s Christmas retelling of Jane Austen's Persuasion, rel. December 2025)

www.ingramcontent.com/pod-product-compliance
Ingram Content Group UK Ltd.
Pitfield, Milton Keynes, MK11 3LW, UK
UKHW061223180426
11947UKWH00027B/1981